My
Dear
Duchess

My Dear Duchess

Marion Chesney

Thorndike Press • Chivers Press
Thorndike, Maine USA   Bath, England

This Large Print edition is published by Thorndike Press, USA and by Chivers Press, England.

Published in 2001 in the U.S. by arrangement with NAL Signet, a division of Penguin Putnam Inc.

Published in 2001 in the U.K. by arrangement with the author.

U.S. Hardcover 0-7862-3362-1 (Basic Series Edition)
U.K. Hardcover 0-7540-4553-6 (Chivers Large Print)
U.K. Softcover   0-7540-4554-4 (Camden Large Print)

The text of this Large Print edition is unabridged.
Other aspects of the book may vary from the original edition.

Set in 16 pt. Plantin by Elena Picard.

Printed in the United States on permanent paper.

British Library Cataloguing-in-Publication Data available

Library of Congress Cataloging-in-Publication Data

Chesney, Marion.
　　My dear duchess / by Marion Chesney.
　　　　p.　cm.
　　ISBN 0-7862-3362-1 (lg. print : hc : alk. paper)
　　1. Inheritance and succession — Fiction. 2. Married people — Fiction. 3. Runaways — Fiction. 4. Nobility — Fiction. 5. Large type books. I. Title.
　　PR6053.H4535 M92 2001
　　823'.914—dc21
　　　　　　　　　　　　　　　　　　　　2001023696

My
Dear
Duchess

Chapter One

Everyone in the top ten thousand agreed that the weather was no respecter of persons. A heavy rain roared down on London town with unremitting violence, chuckling in the lead gutters, pouring down the drainpipes and setting the filth from the kennels awash over the roads. The Season had begun but two weeks ago and now the promising groundwork that had been assiduously laid by hopeful mothers and their equally hopeful daughters seemed to be in a fair way to being ruined. Rides in the park at the fashionable hour, shopping in Bond Street, ices at Gunters — the myriad of opportunities for chance encounters to further the acquaintance of the ballroom — were all being washed away.

Even Clarence Square, the most fashionable of Mayfair addresses, had not escaped the ravages of the deluge. Water soaked into the brick facade of its elegant buildings and ran in little waterfalls from its stately porticos. The pretty gardens of the square were pockmarked by huge depressing puddles and the battered rose bushes threw their scarlet petals over the sodden grass like summer warriors bleeding to death before an onslaught of watery spears.

Captain Henry Wright jolted into the square in the confines of a stuffy carriage and fretted for the hundredth time in the cage that was called love. Instead of putting on the gloves with his friends at Jackson's or playing a rubber of piquet at White's, here he was, all dressed up like a Bond Street fribble in a coat with twelve shoulder capes and buttons the size of soup plates, going to call on a young female and endure the cold glances of her odious mother.

Ever since he had set eyes on Clarissa Sayers but a se'enight ago at her come-out ball, his heart had been lost — to the great amazement of London society who had labelled the Captain a hardened flirt. His sister, Emily, could point out that Mrs. Sayers, whose vast fortune came from a series of thriving woolen manufactures in the North, smelled of the shop and was an encroaching Cit. His friends could remind him that since he had just been honorably discharged with a leg wound after the long rigors of the Peninsular War, he was bound to be susceptible and ready to fall for the first pretty face he met. But all in vain. He had no sooner set eyes on Clarissa's ethereal beauty than his heart was well and truly hers.

His goddess preferred the Dandy set rather than the athletic Corinthians that the Captain favored — hence the outrageous coat which was already beginning to make him feel uncomfortable.

In spite of the drenching rain, he walked slowly up the wide marble steps and then banged on the knocker with unnecessary violence. He was admitted by the butler and, with relief, was divested of his outer coat. Revealed underneath was an impeccable swallow tail coat which might meet with the butler's approval, but he felt sure that his love would have been better pleased had he attired himself in all the glory of padded shoulders and a nipped waist.

His heart beating fast, the Captain followed the butler up the wide carpeted stairs to a morning room on the first floor and, straightening his cravat and feeling like a schoolboy, made his entrance.

But there was nothing in his manner to betray his feelings to Miss Clarissa Sayers or to her mother who were engaged at their embroidery. From his fair curly hair cut in a fashionable Brutus crop to his shiny hessians with their little gold tassles, he was the epitome of languid elegance.

Mrs. Sayers was a plump woman of middle years dressed in a green and white striped dress displaying a generous expanse of mottled bosom. An elaborate lace cap was balanced precariously on curls of an improbable gold. Her heavy jaw betrayed all the force of character that was necessary for a matron, however rich, with a background of trade, to storm the aristocratic bastions of London's West End. She hid her heavy domineering character behind a mask of helpless girlish fluttering. When her bluff Yorkshire husband had departed this world in a fit of apoplexy she lost no time, once the regulation period of mourning was over, to realize her lifelong ambition. Her beautiful daughter should make her debut in London and marry a title. No less than a Lord would suffice. And with her fortune and Clarissa's looks, she was in no doubt that she would soon succeed. She had paid a certain "lady of quality" handsomely to assure her daughter's entree into the best circles and only certain hostesses, notoriously high in the instep, had kept their doors firmly closed.

She eyed the handsome Captain with a gleam of disfavor which she hurriedly masked by ringing the bell for refreshments. After all, the Captain moved in the first circles and his father's death had assured him of an easy competence. And she had no fear of her darling throwing herself away. Clarissa was as ambitious to secure a title as her mama.

Clarissa betrayed none of her ambitions, however as she smiled prettily at the Captain and thanked him in her soft voice for having ventured out in such terrible weather.

"I am sure no one else would have been so *brave*," she smiled, flashing a melting look at Captain Wright. As usual, he was so taken aback by her beauty that he scarcely heard what she said. Her hair, as fair as his own, rioted over her small head in artistic disorder. Her gown of blue-figured muslin complemented wide blue eyes set in a small heart-shaped face. The slightest gesture she made from the turn of her wrist to the way she applied neat stitches in the tambour frame in front of her was poetry in motion.

"Now you'll be turning our poor young Captain's head," fluttered Mrs. Sayers. "You know the Earl of Minster and the Marquis of Blandhaven are to call. I declare my child has so many handsome beaux Mr. Wright, it quite makes me worry which she is going to choose."

"I hope she chooses from the heart," said the Captain lightly.

"But *of course* I will," said Clarissa, opening wide her blue eyes which seemed to hold a meaning for the Captain alone. "*You* at least do not think that titles mean anything to me, my dear Mr. Wright."

A footman arrived with the tea tray and the Captain took the opportunity to lean closer to Clarissa. "Does that mean there is hope for me, Miss Sayers?" he asked in a light, teasing voice. But when she looked up into his grey eyes what she saw there made her heart beat faster with a pleasant sensation of power. She would ensnare him further. Broken hearts could only add to a debutante's consequence, and the handsome Captain was quite a catch.

"Of course you may hope," she whispered with a cautious eye on her mother who was busy with the tea things out of earshot at the other side of the room.

"Miss Sayers," he said with a hard edge to his voice. "Do not flirt with me, I beg . . ."

"Flirt?" Clarissa turned a pretty muslin shoulder on him. "You do me great wrong. I never *flirt*."

She turned back and cast a look up at him through her lashes. He was watching her with a fierce speculation in his gaze which for a moment gave the belle pause. Perhaps . . . just perhaps . . . this Captain who exuded such a strong air of commanding masculinity might prove more than she could handle. Then she mentally shrugged. There had never been any man in her young life that she had been unable to manage.

Mrs. Sayers bustled back and began coyly making pleasantries in such an arch manner that the Captain could only wonder how the vulgar creature could have produced such an exquisite daughter.

When he finally rose to take his leave, he enquired of the ladies if he might expect to see them at the opera that evening. Gasparo Pacchierotti, the male soprano, was to sing. "Oh, dear," simpered Mrs. Sayers with a quick look at her daughter, "I think since the weather is so dreadful, that perhaps we shall sit quietly at home. But we shall certainly be with Mrs. Bannington's party at Vauxhall on the morrow."

He bowed. "Pray do not ring for the servant, madam. I can find my way," he said. Clarissa raised her eyes to his in farewell. They seemed to hold a message of warmth meant for himself alone. Already dreading the long wait until the following evening, he closed the door behind him and stood for a few moments on the landing. Should he have pressed them to accompany him to the opera? The message in Clarissa's eyes had been unmistakable and no young girl that he had ever met would look just that way at a man unless her affections were engaged.

A drop of moisture fell on his hand and he stared at it in a puzzled way. The roof must be leaking. It was followed by another drop. He looked upwards.

A child's face stared sadly and solemnly down at him from an upper landing. He raised his hand in mock salute and prepared to descend the stairs.

A small hiccupping sob stopped him in his tracks.

Moved by a kindly impulse he turned about and mounted with easy athletic steps to the upper floor. Crouching beside the bannisters in the shadowy light of the stairwell was a young girl. Her long, black hair fell straight to her waist and she was dressed in a short, faded tarlatan gown. He thought her to be about fourteen. He put his long fingers under her chin and turned the tear-stained face up to his.

"Why so mournful, miss," he said gently. "Is there not enough water already on this dreadful day?"

Large black eyes flecked with golden light held his own for a moment and then dropped. "It's of no use," sobbed the pathetic figure. "I shall live in the schoolroom till I die."

"Surely a few years is not so long," he said teasingly.

The girl got to her feet. "I am seventeen years of age," she said with a quaint dignity, "and until Clarissa gets married I'm condemned to remain up here."

"Clarissa! Why? How should that affect you, my child?" asked the Captain intrigued.

"I am determined to introduce myself," said the girl, smoothing down her faded gown, "I am Miss Frederica Sayers and you are Captain Henry Wright." She went on as he would have interrupted her. "You see I know everyone who calls. I see them from the top of the stairs, although it's very difficult telling what people are like by just the top of their heads."

"But why must Clarissa be married before you descend the stairs?" pursued the Captain, looking down at her. No wonder he had taken her for a child. She was barely five feet tall!

"Oh, please come into the schoolroom where we can talk," said Frederica. "Someone's coming."

The bewildered Captain found himself whisked into the schoolroom and the door

15

shut behind him. It was a small, depressing room with a sanded floor and furnished with a deal table and two upright chairs. Small barred windows let in the dull grey light of the murky day outside. His petite hostess jerked forward one of the hard chairs and motioned him to sit, perching herself on the other and gazing at him with wide eyes. She began without preamble. "It's like this. Mama says I am a troublesome *ingenue* and that I would only embarrass Clarissa if I appeared in public and that poor Clarissa has waited a long time for this Season since she is already two and twenty."

The Captain looked at her and raised his thin brows. "I am surprised your sister is not yet wed. It does not say much for the young bloods of Yorkshire."

"Oh, she had offers a-plenty but she didn't want any of them. She wanted to have a Season and marry a title but Papa said there was nothing wrong with Yorkshire and she should stay there . . . but . . . then he died and Mama said she would see to it that Clarissa was rewarded."

"I fear you are confusing your mama's ambitions with those of your sister," commented the Captain acidly. It was only natural after all that this embarrassing chit

16

should be jealous of her beautiful sister.

"Are you in love with her?" asked Frederica, looking at him with those large and strange eyes.

"Yes," he said baldly, suddenly wishing himself elsewhere.

"It's only natural," she sighed. "I will help you if you will help me. I can tell you . . . oh . . . all sorts of useful things. For example, they are going to the opera tonight."

"But Mrs. Sayers assured me . . ."

"To the opera," she went on firmly. "Mama wants her to make a match with the Marquis of Blandhaven but Clarissa is a bit frightened of him because he's said to be a roue and to keep a string of West End Comets."

"Watch your tongue, miss," said the Captain beginning to sympathize with Mrs. Sayers.

"*And* so if you were to go to the opera, say, around about the last act, I think you could be sure of a welcome from Clarissa."

"Thank you for your information," he said dryly, "but I am perfectly capable of carrying on a courtship without your help."

Two tears began to form in Frederica's eyes. "Oh, what's the use," she sobbed. "Now you won't help me."

17

The Captain levelled his quizzing glass at the woebegone figure and sighed. "How can I be of assistance, Miss Frederica?"

She looked at him pathetically through her tears. "I . . . I was hoping you could help *bring me out*. Mama is taking me with her on a shopping expedition to Bond Street at ten o'clock tomorrow. If you were to meet us by chance and demand an introduction and *then* say that you hope to see me at Mrs. Bannington's party at Vauxhall *then* mama might be persuaded to take me. I do so long to see Vauxhall. *Please*. You have no idea what it is like to hear the sounds of all the music and parties and never, ever, be able to join in. *Please*."

"Very well, then," said the Captain, after a moment's reflection. It would do no harm, he decided, to befriend Clarissa's little sister. Keeping the child in the schoolroom was surely entirely Mrs. Sayers' idea. Clarissa on the other hand would be grateful to him for being kind to her sister.

She flew out of her chair and flung her arms around his neck and planted a resounding kiss on his cheek.

"Oh *thank you*," she breathed. "Oh, how I wish . . ."

"What do you wish, my child?" he teased, tugging at a lock of her long hair.

18

"Why . . . I wish that the sun may shine tomorrow," she laughed.

But after the tall figure of the Captain had descended the stairs, Miss Frederica Sayers whispered to the uncaring schoolroom walls, "Oh, Captain Henry Wright. *How* I wish you were in love with *me*."

Chapter Two

"If you stop once more in the middle of the pavement, I shall take you home directly," stormed Mrs. Sayers, pushing her youngest daughter in front of her along Bond Street and thanking her stars that the hour was too early to attract any fashionable shoppers.

Mrs. Sayers was out of sorts. Who would have thought that Captain Wright would attend the opera last night after all. And who would have thought that her usually biddable daughter would cold shoulder the Marquis at the second interval to flirt with the Captain. And now *this* ridiculous daughter of hers was mooning along like a *widgeon* looking for all the world as though she had lost something precious.

The sun shone down so brightly on the rainwashed street that at moments it seemed as if London was indeed paved with gold. Tiny wisps of clouds, the tattered stragglers from yesterday's storm, chased each other across a sky of pure cerulean.

Mrs. Sayers stopped to admire a dashing bonnet of pleated lilac silk in a milliner's window. She was often to remember that had it not been for the wretched bonnet, she could have been half way down Piccadilly before disaster befell.

A polite "Good morning, ma'am" brought her about and she stared upwards in dismay into the tanned and smiling face of Captain Wright. And as if that were not enough, hanging on his arm, her face alight with mischief was none other than that dashing society matron, Mrs. Bannington — she who had invited the Sayers to Vauxhall that very evening.

Her thoughts running like rats about her brain, Mrs. Sayers gushed, "Good morning Mrs. Bannington . . . Captain Wright. Get behind me, girl!" The latter was hissed in an undertone to Frederica. If her daughter stood meekly and silently behind her, then Mrs. Sayers fervently hoped that Frederica might be taken for the maid. But that wretched child stayed exactly where she was, smiling at the Captain and Mrs. Bannington and patiently waiting for an introduction.

Mrs. Sayers made a supreme effort to extricate herself but Mrs. Bannington had already taken Frederica's hand in her own. "And who have we here?" she demanded.

Frederica saw her golden chance and took

it. Without waiting for her mother, she smiled at Mrs. Bannington, "I am Frederica Sayers."

"Indeed!" cried Mrs. Bannington, her thin pencilled brows almost vanishing into her hair. "A cousin of Clarissa's perhaps."

"No ma'am, her younger sister," said Frederica, nervously aware of the seething volcano that was her mother standing beside her.

"Indeed," said Mrs. Bannington again. "You know Captain Wright perhaps?" And without waiting for a reply, she presented Frederica. His grey eyes held a mocking look but he bowed over her hand and then addressed himself to the angry Mrs. Sayers, "I was not aware that you had *two* beautiful daughters."

"Tish. Frederica is but a schoolgirl. Now if you . . ."

"I am seventeen, mama," Frederica reminded her with a sweet smile.

"Seventeen! Oh, you must not keep her hidden," said Mrs. Bannington. "I insist that you bring Frederica to Vauxhall tonight."

Mrs. Sayers' face was a study. Mrs. Bannington was one of London's foremost hostesses and her voice had held an undoubted steely note of command. To exclude Frederica from the outing would be to exclude Clarissa from any future Banning-ton entertainments. Mrs. Sayers' thin mouth curved down to meet her massive jaw. She looked remarkably like an irritated bulldog. "Very well, then," she said with bad grace. She had an obscure feeling that this was all the fault of Captain Wright. She suddenly saw a way in which she could make some use of this social disaster. Mrs. Sayers smiled sweetly on Mrs. Bannington. The bulldog had just found a juicy bone in unpromising ground. She said:

"Perhaps you could be of some service to me this evening, Captain Wright. You know how it is at these Vauxhall parties. Everyone swears to stick together and not get lost and then as soon as they're through the gates, they start pairing off and one never sees anyone again until after the fireworks. Would you be so kind as to keep an eye on my little Frederica? A *fatherly* eye, of course. It is all right for Clarissa. She never wants for beaux but poor little Frederica will need some gentleman to take care of her."

There was nothing Captain Wright could do but bow and say he would be delighted. It said a lot for his breeding and social charm that he managed to leave Mrs. Sayers with the impression that he was indeed as pleased as he said.

23

But as Mrs. Sayers and Frederica turned the corner, he looked ruefully down at Mrs. Bannington, "I fear I have underestimated Mrs. Sayers. What a horrible Friday-faced female she is. How she could contrive to produce so beautiful a daughter as Clarissa is beyond me."

"Or Frederica for that matter," said Mrs. Bannington. "Oh, don't look so surprised. I'll swear that girl has more character in her little finger than your precious Clarissa any day. I know it is hard to judge when she is wearing a shapeless dress and that quiz of a bonnet, but I swear if the chit were dressed properly, she could set London by the ears."

"She's a child," said the Captain, wearying of the subject. "But I am grateful to you, ma'am, for helping to *bring her out*,' as she put it. I must confess I like my beauties to be a little more mature." His mocking smile glinted down at her, appraising her smart scarlet walking dress and dashing shako set saucily on her red curls. Mrs. Bannington was a widow in her middle thirties and very happy with her single state. But the handsome Captain was one of her favorites and as she smiled back, she wondered again why such a sophisticated man-about-town could lose his heart to a cardboard miss like Clarissa Sayers.

★ ★ ★

The cardboard miss was yawning over the breakfast table when Frederica and her mother came in — or rather when Frederica was propelled into the room by a series of pokes and pushes from the irate Mrs. Sayers.

"There will be no end of tittle-tattle when *this* gets around the town, miss!" cried Mrs. Sayers, thrusting her packages into the arms of a waiting footman. "Your young sister *introduced* herself as bold as brass to Mrs. Bannington. *And* Captain Wright. What is more the saucy minx has *compelled* Sally Bannington to invite her to Vauxhall tonight."

"Why in such a pucker," yawned Clarissa. Her glance flicked contemptuously over the tiny figure of her sister from her braided hair to her tiny feet. "You do not expect the shine to be taken out of me by *Frederica*."

"No, indeed," cried her fond mother. "But she looks so young."

"You refine too much on it, mama," said Clarissa in a bored voice. "Nothing troubles me because I am beautiful. There is no one in the whole of London as beautiful as I. Nor will there be." She delivered herself of this piece of self-praise with a calm vanity quite awful to behold. "Put the chit's hair up and lend her one of my gowns. She'll look old enough then I warrant you."

"Well, I declare I am glad you are taking it so well," declared Mrs. Sayers. "But I made sure that you should enjoy the company of the Marquis tonight without interruption. I requested that Captain Wright should devote his time to Frederica."

"What a ninnyhammer you are," laughed Clarissa. "Nothing will keep the gallant Captain from my side, especially not my dear sister."

"Don't be too sure of that," cried the much-goaded Frederica.

"Listen to the little girl," teased Clarissa with maddening good nature. She rose lazily to her feet and pinched her little sister painfully on the cheek.

"You are so shy, Frederica, you know you will blush and stammer every time a gentleman so much as looks at you. But be warned. Stick by mama. The Captain will not give you above a minute of his time."

But as the carriages rattled over Westminster Bridge that evening on the road to the Royal Gardens, Clarissa eyed her little sister with something approaching dislike. Mrs. Sayers' attempt to age Frederica had only succeeded in turning the chit into a pretty young woman. Her masses of jet black hair had been dressed high on her small head in a fashion that was all her own. Instead of attiring her in any of the pastels considered suitable for a young debutante, colors which would have made Frederica's olive skin look sallow, she had found her an old rose crepe gown of Clarissa's which made her skin the color of light gold. Simple gold jewelery brought out the gold flecks in her large eyes and the only small comfort Clarissa had was that the child was too short for beauty.

Captain Wright smiled at the animated little face opposite him in the carriage. He had been regretting his generous impulse since the very sight of Frederica seemed to put his beloved out of sorts, but he had to admit that Frederica's happiness was infectious.

Even the languid and elegant Marquis of Blandhaven seemed to be charmed by the girl. He was paying her extravagant compliments while Frederica laughed with delight, seemingly oblivious to her mother's warning frowns or her elder sister's displeasure.

They arrived at the gate to the gardens and the Captain prepared to gallantly offer Frederica his escort but the Marquis was already there before him, proferring his arm and leading her along the walk. The Captain gladly offered his arm to the fair Clarissa but he watched the pair ahead of him with a worried frown.

Lord Percival, Marquis of Blandhaven, was not a gentleman that any mama should trust. A notorious member of the Dandy Set from his padded shoulders to his high heeled shoes, he was considered to be of the first stare by a certain section of society who considered the Corinthians too sober and austere in their dress. He was a man of five-and-thirty and his hard, thin features under their delicate layer of paint were considered handsome enough. But there were too many unsavory rumors attached to his name. He was reputed to have a passion for very young girls.

"I feel that your sister should not be left alone with Blandhaven," he confided to Clarissa as he escorted her to Mrs. Bannington's box.

She gave a rippling laugh and rapped him playfully with her fan. "I declare you are jealous, sir!" she cried. "But do not waste your time worrying about Frederica. Lord Percival is only devoting his time to her to *please me*."

The Captain turned to look down at her, slightly astonished at the arrogance of her remark, but as they had just come into the lights of hundreds of lanterns, and

Clarissa's perfect face turned up to his was such a vision of beauty, he felt his breath catch in his throat and completely forgot what she had just said.

Frederica was unheeding of her escort's compliments. For Vauxhall was like a fairytale come true — the myriads of lamps, the musicians in their cocked hats who played in a golden cockleshell in the center of the gardens, the servants in shabby liveries carrying pots of stout, the bouncing dances of the cockneys, and above all the twinkling boxes where one could dine on almost invisible wafers of ham and perhaps exchange a few commonplaces with the handsome Captain.

The Marquis had ordered a bowl of rack punch. Mrs. Bannington was drinking champagne and advised Frederica in an undertone to do the same "for that nasty aniseed-flavored punch can really make one feel quite unwell."

The rack punch, however, seemed to have quite an enervating effect on Clarissa so that when the bell rang for the fireworks display, she merely shrugged when she heard the Marquis asking her mother's permission to take Frederica to the show. Mrs. Sayers bit her lip in vexation but was still too overawed by anyone who held a title to demure. Frederica was so excited that she would not have cared who escorted her.

Oblivious of the Marquis, she oohed and aaahed with the best of them as the myriads of stars exploded and cascaded over the gardens. The final fiery tableau of "God Bless The Prince of Wales" brought the exhibition to a close and with a tremulous sigh of satisfaction, she turned to her aristocratic companion.

He was looking down at her with an unreadable expression in his eyes. "Come, Miss Frederica, and I shall take you back to our box," he said, holding her arm in an unnecessarily tight grip.

He led her along a dark walk away from the lights and slid an arm around her waist. Frederica came to an abrupt halt. "My Lord Marquis," she said firmly. "Please remove your arm. It is not at all proper."

An insolent laugh greeted her words and he drew her into an arbor. "My prim schoolroom miss," he whispered. "The most exciting things in life are not at all proper." And before she could break away, he had forced his mouth down on hers, enveloping her in a suffocating halitosis of rack punch and decaying teeth.

Unaware of how Miss Frederica Sayers

was being brought out, Captain Wright walked slowly along an adjoining walk with Clarissa. She leaned heavily on his arm and her eyes were like stars. Clarissa had never drunk anything as heady as the rack punch before and she was toying with the idea of letting the Captain steal a kiss. Vauxhall was practically the only place where one could walk with a gentleman without a maid or one's mama in constant attendance. She stole a look at her companion. After the disastrous purchase of the coat which the Captain had bestowed upon his valet, he had resolved that he could never aspire to the Dandy Set and was dressed in severe black and white evening dress. He really was so handsome, sighed Clarissa to herself. Such a pity he did not have a title. But one little kiss did not make a marriage. She leaned more heavily on his arm and then let out a mock squeal of alarm.

"What is the matter?" asked the Captain, coming to a halt.

"It is nothing," said Clarissa, placing her hands on his chest and staring up into his face. To her disappointment, Captain Wright made as if to move on. He needed more encouragement. She slid her arms round his neck.

He looked down at her in surprise. Her

beautiful face was turned upwards to his in the faint moonlight. Very slowly, he bent his head and kissed her. Her lips were warm and clinging but, somewhere in the back of his brain, he was just beginning to register with surprise that absolutely nothing seemed to be happening to his senses, when he clearly and distinctly heard his name being called.

A high, thin, childish wail of fright penetrated the night air. "Oh, help! Captain Wright ... somebody ... help!"

He put Clarissa from him and looked around wildly. The sound had come from the adjoining walk. "Your sister!" he cried. Fortunately for Clarissa, he was too worried to see his fair partner's shrug or hear her indifferent comment of "So?" Dragging Clarissa with him, he ran headlong through the bushes.

There in the shadowy light, he could just make out the small figure of Frederica struggling in the Marquis of Blandhaven's arms. With an oath, he strode forward and sent the Marquis flying backwards into the bushes with a well-placed hit.

"A mill! A mill!" cried several voices and suddenly the walk seemed to be alive with people.

Clarissa stamped her foot. She had never

been so angry in her life. "Take me back to Mrs. Bannington's box immediately, sir!" she cried to Captain Wright. "How dare you subject me to the vulgar gaze of these common people."

The Marquis had disappeared. Frederica was trembling and gazing up at the Captain with adoring eyes. "A flush hit," she breathed. "Oh, *what* a facer you landed him, Captain Wright!"

Clarissa's voice dripped ice. "If you have finished talking *cant,* Freddie, perhaps someone may pay attention to *me.* My dress is in ruins. I have unceremoniously been *dragged* through the bushes without so much as a by-your-leave and all because my little sister has been encouraging the advances of poor Lord Percival. This is what becomes of introducing provincial hoydens to society."

"Fustian!" cried Frederica, made bold by her adoration of the Captain. "Go take a damper."

The much overwrought Clarissa darted forward and boxed her sister's ears and then burst out into noisy tears.

"Pray control yourself, Miss Sayers," said the Captain in a calm voice. "You do not want to spoil those beautiful eyes by making them red." This and the fact that the Captain was looking at her in a new speculative way, had the effect of making Clarissa dry her tears. She did not want to lose an admirer. She hugged Frederica and apologized in a pretty, soft voice which had the desired effect of bringing the warmth back to the Captain's eyes. And only Frederica was aware of the vicious pinch on the arm which Clarissa gave her as they approached the box.

Once again the Captain had to go to Frederica's rescue. Mrs. Sayers would not believe that a *Marquis* could be capable of any misconduct. By the time he had soothed her the Captain felt considerably older. Then as he caught Clarissa's eye, he noticed that she was looking at him with that particular intimacy which she seemed to share with him alone.

He bent over Clarissa's hand at the end of the evening. "I shall call on your mama in the morning," he whispered softly.

Clarissa immediately cast down her eyes but the Captain put it down to maidenly modesty and, well-satisfied, took his leave.

Frederica had caught the whisper and wondered if she could possibly reach the privacy of her bedroom before she burst into tears.

Chapter Three

It had never dawned on the Captain that Mrs. Sayers might be absent from home on the following morning. The butler showed him into the downstairs drawing room, volunteering the information that Miss Sayers was at home.

The Captain paced up and down nervously, feeling as if he were in some kind of exotic, striped cage. Broad crimson and gold stripes embellished the upholstery, broad crimson and gold strips raced up and down the wallpaper and barred the heavy curtains. A French landscape portraying a long country road lined with poplars was hung above the fireplace to add the finishing touch to the horizontal effect. Mrs. Sayers had forgotten the color scheme at floor level and Chinese rugs in delicate blues and whites seemed to cringe before their noisier rivals.

He turned abruptly as the butler announced Clarissa and then retired leaving the door punctiliously open. With a fast-beating heart, the Captain strode forward and took her hand. She had faint blue shadows under her eyes which seemed to enhance her fragile beauty rather than detract from it.

Captain Wright made a move to take her into his arms but she retreated a step and said in a cold voice, "State your business, sir. I am engaged to drive with Lord Percival this morning."

"What!" cried the Captain, outraged. "After last night. How could you, Clarissa?"

"I was not aware that I had given you permission to use my Christian name," she retorted in chilly accents.

The Captain shook his head in a baffled kind of way. This was not going at all the way he had planned. Then he suddenly smiled. Of course! She was just as nervous as he!

He led the reluctant girl to the sofa and sat beside her and began, "After last night, Miss Sayers, I am no longer in any doubt that my feelings are reciprocated. Will you do me the inestimable honor of accepting my hand in marriage?"

She bowed her head and traced the pattern in the rug with one slippered foot.

"No," she said baldly.

"But, my dear . . ." began the Captain.

Clarissa got to her feet. "My dear sir," she said lightly and hurriedly, "I fear you have placed too much importance on a stolen kiss by moonlight. I am extremely honored by your proposal but," here she stifled a yawn, "I infinitely regret I cannot accept it."

"May I hope that you may change your mind?" said the Captain stiffly.

Clarissa stole a look at him from under her lashes. He was so handsome. She was tempted to keep him dancing on her string. But then her pretty face hardened. He deserved to be punished for dragging her through the bushes in that hurly-burly way.

The spiteful side of her nature, of which only Frederica was aware, surfaced. Rising to her feet she tugged at the bellrope, and then turned to him, her face alight with an almost hellish amusement.

"I did not remain unwed this long, my dear sir, in order to throw myself away on a mere *Captain*. Me! Plain Mrs. Wright to end my days serving tea to your boring regimental friends and their boring little wives. I shall be my Lady Clarissa and I shall settle for no less."

Captain Wright clenched his fists. He had a sudden overwhelming desire to slap her hard. The hard, vindictive face before him was so unlike that of the soft and beautiful girl he knew that he half wondered if he were going mad.

He gathered the rags of his dignity. "I give you good day, ma'am," he said, making his best bow. The sound of Clarissa's icy, mocking laughter rang in his ears as he left the house, and seemed to follow him all the way across Clarence Square.

Clarissa yawned and stretched like a cat as she moved slowly up the stairs to prepare for her morning's drive. She found herself confronted on the upper landing by Frederica. The girl was trembling and faced her with a desperate appeal in her wide eyes.

Clarissa smiled wickedly and gave her little sister's hair a playful yank. "Oh, you should have seen the so-dear Captain," she trilled. "Turned down flat. I left him on his knees, Frederica. Crying, actually crying. Me, marry that nobody! Such presumption. He would do very well for you, of course. But who would look at *you* after *me*."

Frederica did what the Captain had wanted to do — she gave her beautiful sister a resounding slap across the face. Clarissa promptly went into strong hysterics, accentuated by the sound of her mother's arrival.

Frederica was given six of the best with the birch rod and locked in the schoolroom, after which energetic effort Mrs. Sayers turned her energies to soothing Clarissa and telling her she had done just as she ought.

The cause of all this drama strode into his lodgings in Harvey Street — apparently deaf to his man's entreaties that he had visitors — and into the living room where he hurled his riding crop into the corner and roared for the decanter. His friend, Lord Archibald Hefford, uncoiled his length from the armchair and stared at the Captain in dismay. "Never say she refused you!" he declared in amazement.

The Captain tossed down a bumper of brandy and collapsed into the chair opposite. "The fair Clarissa not only refused me. She enjoyed doing so. She is hanging out for a title. Made no bones about it, Archie! You should have heard the hell cat. How on earth could I have been so blind? How could I have been such a damned fool?"

"You never saw past her beauty," said his friend simply. "I can't blame you either, the way that minx was making up to you. And you could have had your pick of any female in London without patronizing the mushroom class. Is your heart broken?"

Captain Wright gave him a sudden rueful smile. "No. That is still intact. But I swear to you, Archie, my pride has taken a hell of a beating."

"I ain't much in the petticoat line," said

Lord Hefford slowly, "but I swear to God, Henry, I would like to make a play for that chit and then jilt her."

The Captain looked at his friend with affection. As dark as the Captain was fair, Lord Hefford was a Top-Of-The-Trees Corinthian and a clipping rider to hounds. He could drive to an inch and pop a flush hit over no less than the famous Jackson's guard as well as being possessed of a handsome face, figure and fortune. But the Captain shook his head. "You'd need to rig yourself out like a Jack-a-Dandy before she'd look your way. She favors the Tulips and the Bond Street beaux."

"But I have the title," grinned Lord Hefford. "I think I may just lay siege to the fair beauty."

The Captain sighed. "Did you ever read Mary Wollstonecraft's '*A Vindication of the Rights of Woman*'? No? Well, I wish the gentler sex did have the same rights as men at this moment for I would surely call the beautiful Miss Sayers out!"

He turned round at a discreet cough from his gentleman's gentleman, Stubbs, "I have been endeavouring to inform you, sir, that there are three persons awaiting your pleasure in the back parlor."

"Duns?" queried Lord Hefford, looking

alarmed, "You ain't in 'queer street,' Henry?"

"Not yet," he grinned.

Stubbs coughed again. "I believe the gentlemen to be of the legal class. They said the matter they had to discuss with you was of national importance."

The Captain made his way through to the adjoining parlor, leaving his friend with the decanter.

Three middle-aged gentlemen in sober black suits and old-fashioned bagwigs arose at his entrance and bowed so low that their heads nearly touched the ground. The fattest of the three seemed to be elected spokesman. "My lord Duke," he began, "we represent the firm of Rundell, Bruton and Sims. I am Mr. Rundell, on my left is Mr. Bruton and on my right is Mr. Sims. We have called to inform Your Grace . . ."

"Hold hard," said the Captain. "You have come to the wrong address. I am Captain Henry Wright, late of the Seventh Hussars and . . ."

"Just so," interrupted Mr. Rundell. "We . . . ah . . . are . . . um . . . aware . . . of the . . . ah . . . er . . . fact, Your Grace. We have here the will of the late Duke of Westerland, your distant relative. You are no doubt aware that since the late Duke had no offspring and no nearer kin, that you er, succeed to the . . . ah . . . title."

"There must be some mistake . . ."

"Oh, no, Your . . . ah . . . Grace," said Mr. Rundell, crackling a piece of parchment. "No mistake at all! *You* are the new Duke of Westerland."

The Captain . . . or rather the new Duke of Westerland . . . began to laugh, much to the surprise of the three lawyers. What, thought His Grace, was Miss Clarissa Sayers going to think now!

Blissfully unaware of the aristocratic plum that had just escaped her clutches, Clarissa returned from her drive to find Mrs. Sayers in a high flutter.

The "lady of quality," bribed heavily by Mrs. Sayers to effect social entree into all drawing rooms, a Mrs. Byles-Bondish, sat unmoved on the striped sofa.

As Clarissa entered the room, Mrs. Byles-Bondish was saying, "I am afraid that is the case, ma'am. I know you are desirous of Clarissa's attending the Falconer ball since only *the creme de la creme* will be admitted. But this morning, Lady Falconer made it exceeding plain that she wished Frederica to attend. Lady Falconer is as close as inkleweavers with Mrs. Bannington. Furthermore my lady implied that unless Frederica were to be present, no invitation would be issued to the Sayers family."

"It's all on account of that spiteful cat, Mary Bannington," said Clarissa carelessly.

"It fair chokes me to think of that brat waltzing around the Falconer's ball," said Mrs. Sayers with barely controlled venom.

Mrs. Byles-Bondish raised her thin eyebrows in surprise. "My dear Mrs. Sayers," she drawled. "One would not think that Frederica was your daughter."

Mrs. Sayers bit her lip in vexation and exchanged glances with her daughter. Clarissa opened her mouth to burst out with something but a warning look from her mother made her close it again.

Clarissa was still flushed with triumph over her rejection of the Captain. "Oh, let her go," she said. "I will even choose a dress for here. Now pale yellow would be just the thing . . ."

Clarissa, having neatly chosen the most unflattering color for her troublesome sister, settled back to turn over the Captain's humiliation in her mind. She hoped he would be at the ball so that she could enjoy the rejected agony on that handsome face.

At that precise moment the Captain's face

was indeed registering agony, but not over Clarissa. He faced the lawyers who had just finished reading the terms of the will and looked at them in horror.

"Marry! I must marry? It cannot be true."

"I am afraid it is, Your Grace," said Mr. Rundell portentously. "The old Duke was very bitter at the end of his days about having never married. You may inherit the title and the estates but not his personal fortune unless you are married within a month of the reading of the will. And may I point out, Your Grace, you will need to control the fortune in order to run your property efficiently. I am sure that a young gentleman of your looks and address should not find it an impossible task."

After the lawyers had left, the new Duke of Westerland strolled slowly into the living room to impart the staggering news to his friend.

Lord Hefford shook his head. "I don't know whether you're to be congratulated or commiserated with," he said. "Being a Duke ain't easy." A sudden thought struck him. "I'd lay a monkey to see Miss Sayers' face when she finds out."

"That brings me to the hardest part," said the Duke. "I am to be married before the month is out or I don't get the old Duke's fortune."

44

Lord Hefford whistled. "Well, there's plenty that'll have you for your title. You'd best look high for a woman of breeding who can handle the responsibilities of an abbey. What about Lady Rothence, Haswell's daughter?"

"Too proud," said the Duke. "No. Since I obviously cannot fall in love in such a short time, I would prefer some female who would be modest and good company. Some girl who would *grow* into the position as I will have to grow. Good God, Archie. Where shall I find the time? There is a vast pile in Surrey, that great barracks in Grosvenor Square — not to mention a castle in Scotland and various hunting boxes in the North. The old Duke's steward will take a lot of the business off my hands but still . . . dammit, I'll miss all this." He looked round his living room, cluttered with mementoes of his school, army, and sporting days.

Stubbs entered the room with the air of a man who can no longer be surprised. "There is a young lady to see Your Grace. I have put her in the back parlor."

The Duke swung round and regarded his man with astonishment, "Really, Stubbs, you should know better than to . . ."

"A most *respectable* young lady," interrupted Stubbs, "Her maid awaits below stairs."

"News travels fast," shouted Lord Hefford to his friend's already-retreating back. "They'll soon be breaking their ankles on your doorstep, mark my words!"

Primly esconced in the back parlor sat Miss Frederica Sayers. She had removed her bonnet, and the remains of her coiffeur from Vauxhall tumbled about her ears in a sorry mess. She got to her feet at his entrance, closed her eyes firmly and said in a loud voice, "I am come to be your mistress, Captain Wright."

After a short minute, she opened her eyes. The Duke was standing motionless, looking at her as if he could hardly believe his eyes. "Why this sudden decision, Miss Frederica?" he asked politely, drawing up a chair for her.

Frederica sat down suddenly as if her legs had turned to water. "It's no use," she sobbed. "You don't *want* me and I don't know any other gentlemen and I'm too young to be a governess."

The Duke took her small hand in his. "Begin at the beginning," he urged. He was interrupted by the entrance of Stubbs. "I took the liberty of bringing some refreshment for the young lady, Your Grace," he said, placing a tea tray on an occasional table.

Frederica's eyes flew to his face. *"Your Grace...?"*

"Yes, indeed," the Duke assured her. "This is a day of surprises. I have just learned that I am the Duke of Westerland."

His companion brightened. "But that makes such a difference, Ca . . . I mean, Your Grace. *Now* you will be able to help me."

He eyed her narrowly, wondering if she were as designing as her sister but her words disarmed him. "You will have large households," she cried. "And surely in one of them you can introduce me to the housekeeper. I am sure you will need an awful lot of maids — Oh, you do not understand. The Falconer ball was the last straw. For some reason, Lady Falconer insisted I be present and . . . and I am to wear primrose yellow satin. So you see, sir, I *had* to run away."

"What is so dreadful about primrose yellow satin?"

"It makes me look sallow," she said, looking at him in surprise. "Surely you must understand why it was the last straw. The beatings, and being perpetually shut in the schoolroom, were as nothing compared to the indignity of that dress. I thought per-

47

haps you might like me as your mistress but I see you do not. But a maid . . ."

He shook his head in amazement. "I must insist that you drink your tea and return directly to your home. Should anyone have seen you arriving at my lodgings your reputation will indeed be ruined. Mistress! My dear child, you will soon be married and wonder how you ever came to think of such a Gothic plan."

"Who's getting married?" hailed a cheerful voice from the doorway.

Lord Archie Hefford strode into the room, his blue eyes sparkling with curiosity. "No one is getting married," snapped the Duke. "I must ask you to leave, Archie. This is a private matter . . ."

To his horror, his words had already gone unheeded, for the confiding Frederica impressed by the large Corinthian with the merry eyes, launched forth on her story.

"I must say your mama seems to treat you uncommon hard," said Archie as she finished her tale.

"She does not really mean to," replied Frederica. "She is simply ambitious for Clarissa. You see, she is my stepmother. My own mother died when I was very little. She was never spoken of. Our old housekeeper told me she was Spanish and sickly most of the time, hating the Yorkshire climate and pining for Spain. Shortly after her death, my father married the widow of a Leeds' banker. My father did not like it known that my mother was a foreigner so he insisted that his new wife and her daughter Clarissa claim me as their blood kin, and moved us all from Leeds to Harrogate so that no one would know. Under the terms of his will, the fiction is supposed to be carried on, but I am the daughter of the house only on sufferance. I have no hope of being married since my stepmother says she will not waste one penny on me. It is not that she actively dislikes me . . . she simply finds me . . . unnecessary. So I thought of the demimonde . . ."

"And you thought of me, miss," said the Duke severely. "What sort of a loose screw do you think I am to go about seducing respectable young ladies?"

"You need to get married," said Archie, patting her hand. He suddenly turned to his friend, his face alight with mischief. "And damme, if there ain't somebody else in this room who needs to get married."

Both Corinthians slowly looked at Frederica.

She was attired in the shabby tarlatan dress which was too short for her and exposed a pair of much-worn half boots. The two men, both over six feet tall, seemed to fill the small, scantily furnished parlor. In their impeccable swallowtail coats, intricate cravats and glossy hessians, they seemed a glittering world away to poor Frederica. She began to wonder if she were mad. It was such a logical idea at the time. Now she had to admit dismally that she did not want to be anyone's mistress except the Duke's.

He was a Duke! Clarissa would surely accept him now. A large tear began to creep down her cheek.

The Duke put a long finger under her chin and turned her face up to his. "I wonder," he mused aloud. "It might just work."

Then he said briskly, "Leave us, Archie."

The Corinthian hesitated in the doorway. "She's such a little thing, Henry. Be gentle . . ."

"I will. I will," he said impatiently, thrusting his large friend from the room.

He came back to stand in front of her. "It so happens, my dear Miss Frederica, that under the terms of the late Duke's will, I must marry before the month is out.

"Now this is too short a time in which to expect any lady to form a *tendre* for me so it must needs be a marriage of convenience.

You need to escape from the unpleasant circumstances of your home and *I* need a wife."

"But Clarissa will have you *now!*" wailed Frederica.

His face hardened. "I do not wish to be wed to any lady who is only interested in my title. I do not wish to be reminded of my idiocy in that direction."

Frederica faltered, "You do . . . do . . .well, you are not, I trust, thinking of a means to *revenge* yourself on my stepsister?"

Now the Duke was only human, and that delicious thought had certainly entered his mind, but he dismissed it firmly. "I am no longer concerned with your stepsister, Miss Frederica. I am sure we shall rub along together famously." His voice softened, "I am not forcing you, you know. It is quite simple to say 'no.'"

Frederica shuddered as she thought of the scene there would be on her return when her stepmother learned that the Captain had become my lord Duke, and that the despised Frederica had snatched the prize from under Clarissa's nose.

As if reading her thoughts, he said gently, "I see no reason you should return. I can take you to my Aunt Matilda in Hartford Street. She is chaperoning my sister Emily for the Season and you can be married from there. Emily would be glad of some young company. I fear she detests London and would rather be in the country with her horses and dogs. What do you say?"

Frederica suddenly realized that if she did not take this chance, she would never forgive herself. She ignored a little warning voice in her brain which was whispering to her that the Duke might never fall in love with her no matter how married they were. She smiled bravely at him and said, "I would like it above all things. But what will my stepmother say?"

He shrugged. "There is little she can say. My aunt will inform her of your visit. The wedding announcement can come as a surprise. I think . . . yes I really think . . . that we should announce our forthcoming nuptials at the Falconer ball. Now let us tell Archie your news."

He opened the door and called to his friend who came in followed by Stubbs who was bearing a bottle of champagne and three glasses.

"I thought celebrations might be the order of the day," said Lord Hefford cheerfully.

The Duke told him of the plan to escort Frederica to his aunt's house. "Capital!"

said Lord Hefford. "You'll find Emily a great girl. No nonsense about her!"

The description of Emily did indeed seem apt as Frederica was urged forward into the salon in Hartford Street some hours later to meet her new friend. Emily Wright was a tall, bony girl with brown hair scraped back from an angular face. When the party entered, she was sitting reading the Gazette with her *legs crossed.*

Frederica hurriedly averted her eyes from this scandalous lapse of good manners. Emily took the news that Frederica was to be her sister-in-law with indifferent calm. "So long as you don't expect me to talk about clothes and balls and trash like that," was her only comment as she buried her head in the paper again.

"Have you *no* manners?" declared her much-exasperated brother.

"None at all," was the cool rejoinder. "Here's auntie. Aunt Matilda — our Henry's a Duke."

"Come to take a look . . . at what," said a vague, thin woman teetering on the threshold. To the amazed Frederica, Mrs. Cholmley, Henry's Aunt Matilda, seemed so frail and emaciated, it was a wonder she did not blow away. She had slanting eyes of pale grey which gazed upon the world with perpetual and myopic wonder. A pale grey chiffon dress clung to her painfully-thin form. She looked like an elderly and kindly marsh spirit.

"This is Frederica Sayers . . . come to stay," said the Duke.

"To pay what, dear?" said his aunt, smiling kindly. "A dressmaker's bill? Madam Vernée is usually not so importunate. Why I can remember the day. . . ."

"Not pay, *STAY!*" roared her nephew.

"Fey? How odd. Have you Scottish blood, my dear?"

Emily gave a sudden bark of laughter. "Don't strain your vocal cords, Henry. You know there's only one person she understands." She gave the bell pull an energetic tug and a heavy-set butler appeared.

"Stafford. Tell Mrs. Cholmley that Captain Wright has just learned that he is the new Duke of Westerland and that Miss Frederica Sayers and he are to be married and that Miss Sayers is to stay with us until the wedding."

"Very good, miss."

Stafford marched to the center of the salon, placed a tapestried footstool on the middle of the rug and stood up on it. Then he began to declaim in a pulpit voice, "Yea verily, Mrs. Cholmley, let it be known and heard in the land that your nephew here has been heralded throughout the realm as the new Duke of Westerland. Also hear ye that His Grace will take unto him, in holy wedlock, Miss Frederica Sayers, who is to reside in this blessed house until that aforesaid happy event."

"Really, how nice, my dear," said Mrs. Cholmley, patting Frederica's hand while Emily whispered to her, "She only understands anything if it sounds as if it's in church. Stone deaf to anything else."

By the time Frederica was shown to her rooms, she felt exhausted by all the strange conversation and the butler's odd translations. A new wardrobe was to be provided for her, or, as Stafford had put it, "Yea verily, raiment shall be furnished forthwith."

Emily pottered around Frederica's little parlor, picking things up and putting them down. At last she burst out, "You see what it's like here. Aunt Matilda is a dear but it gets so wearing always having to ask Stafford to explain things in that biblical manner. Oh, how I wish we could live in the country all the year round."

"Now that the Cap . . . I mean Henry is a Duke, he'll have lots of places in the country and . . ." began Frederica.

"What's the use," said Emily savagely. "I am supposed to get married. This is my second Season and I'm nigh dead of boredom.

"What is the use of being married anyway . . . one becomes no better than a servant." She blushed. "I am sorry," she said impulsively. "I am not always such a bear and so you shall see. I suppose the fact is that I'm just like any other female. I don't care for propping up the walls in the ballroom. Various well-meaning people tell me I ought to prettify up. But what can be done with this set of features?"

"Oh, a great deal," said Frederica timidly. "I collect our first major engagement is the Falconer ball. *Please,* allow me to choose something for you. I hope you do not consider me impertinent," here she looked at Emily's pale pink muslin, "but I feel if you were to wear something more dashing . . . you could look a most striking girl."

"Buy anything you like," said Emily moodily. "Nothing *I* know of will change *me.*"

Chapter Four

Clarissa nimbly executed the steps of the Cotillion, glancing under her upraised arm at a French clock over the mantle. Eleven o'clock and the Duke had not yet arrived.

The name of the new Duke of Westerland had proved to be one of London's best kept secrets as far as the Sayers were concerned. Experts on the peerage had claimed the new member of the aristocracy to be the Honorable Jack Ferrand. But that gentleman had been gambling heavily in the card room almost since the evening began and showed no signs of laying claim to the title.

"A Duke," thought Clarissa, smiling radiantly at her partner while her mind ran round in circles. "And unmarried, they say. I know I could catch him. If only he would come."

As ever, her mama's thoughts were running along much the same lines as her daughter. Of Frederica she barely thought at all except to be relieved that the brat had been taken off her hands by the nutty Mrs. Cholmley and so far showed no signs of appearing on the social scene.

The Cotillion came to a breathless end and, as the couples separated to find their new partners, a stentorian voice from the top of the curving staircase announced, "His Grace, The Duke of Westerland."

All heads turned. Everyone stared. Clarissa glared as if she could not believe her eyes. It was only Captain Wright and that little pest, Frederica. The Duke must be behind them. Where on earth had Frederica found the money to buy that gown?

The pair descended the staircase in stately silence. The Duke was dressed in impeccable black and white with rubies flashing on his cravat and fingers. Frederica wore a flame-red gown of deceptive simplicity cut by the hand of a master to reveal her small and exquisite figure. A thin collar of rubies blazed like fire around her slender throat and her black hair was worn in a coronet.

The waltz was announced, the fiddlers struck up and still Clarissa craned her head. Where was the Duke?

"Magnificent pair aren't they?" murmured a voice at her elbow. Mrs. Bannington was standing beside her, her eyes alight with mischief. "I think Captain Wright looks every inch the Duke."

"Pooh!" said Clarissa rudely. "I am looking for the real Duke."

"But haven't you heard," said Mrs. Bannington with gentle malice. "Captain Wright *is* the Duke."

"Impossible!" shouted Clarissa and then blushed as several people turned to stare at her.

"But not impossible at all," said Mrs. Bannington sweetly. "The Duke and your little sister make such a charming couple." And having delivered her last barb, she drifted off.

Clarissa could feel her heart beating hard against her ribs. Then she relaxed. Of course, all was not lost. Why only last week, he had declared his love for her . . . had asked her to marry him. Well, he should have his wish. That is, if he ever stopped dancing with that little idiot.

But the idiot was still circling in a dream-like trance in the Duke's arms. The Falconers had chosen an Indian theme for their ball. A great tent of white silk was hung from the roof of the ballroom which was so crowded with palm trees, stuffed tigers and exotic plants that it was hard at times for the dancers to find space. The ball was declared to be a sad crush which meant that it was the success of the Season.

Lord Hefford approached Clarissa and begged for a dance but she pleaded fatigue, anxious not to lose a moment of the chase. Archie shrugged and then remembered that he had promised Henry to spare his sister a dance. He searched along the line of wallflowers, looking for the familiar angular figure of Emily Wright, but she was nowhere to be seen. He turned and studied the dance floor. A tall, dashing girl floated past in the arms of her partner and turned to give him a brilliant smile. He smiled back automatically, wondering who the dasher was . . . and then he slowly looked at her again. By George it *was* Emily.

She was wearing a sea-green gown of *crepe* trimmed with bugle beads and cut low to reveal an unexpectedly generous bosom. Gold jewelery flashed at her neck and ears and on the heels of her dancing slippers. Her bony arms were concealed by a pair of long green silk gloves and her gown had a demi-train which added fullness to her figure. He did not know that the precocious Frederica had persuaded Emily to darken her brows and fair eyelashes. Lord Hefford only knew that his childhood friend seemed to have undergone some magical transformation. To blazes with playing games with Clarissa. He would secure Emily for the next dance.

After an hour had passed, Clarissa realized that the Duke was not going to dance with her. He was obviously having his revenge. That did not disturb her. It was exactly how she would have behaved herself.

Resorting to her old tactics, she slipped as she took his hand during the Grand Chain and stumbled against him so heavily that he perforce had to put his arms around her to prevent them both from falling. To Frederica it looked as if he seized hold of Clarissa in an affectionate embrace and her heart sank down to her little scarlet slippers.

She had hardly seen him during a week taken up with the hurried and important affair of choosing a new wardrobe, a project in which Emily had taken an increasing interest, confiding to Frederica that it was so pleasant to shop with someone who could *hear* what one said. Clarissa seemed to be entreating the Duke to remove her from the dance. Frederica momentarily closed her eyes because she could not bear to look. But when she opened them again, the dance was proceeding as if nothing had happened. Clarissa was sitting sulkily beside her mother and the Duke was returning to her round the chain of the dance.

There was a sudden fanfare of trumpets and Lady Falconer mounted a small stage

61

beside the musicians and held up her hands for silence. "My lords, ladies and gentlemen," she cried. "Curiosity has been satisfied. Behold our Duke."

There was much cheering and clapping for Henry Wright was a popular figure. "But this is an evening of surprises," she went on. "Our Duke has chosen his Duchess."

Clarissa let out a little sigh of relief. Who could Lady Falconer mean except herself. Why he had been *crying* with disappointment over her rejection of him. Clarissa had the enviable talent of believing her own lies as soon as she had uttered them. She fixed the Duke with an excited and predatory stare like some exotic bird spying a particularly large and tantalizing worm.

"May I present our future Duchess . . . Miss Frederica Sayers!" said Lady Falconer, holding out her hands to the Duke and Frederica. Blushing at the cries and applause, Frederica mounted the platform with the Duke and then suddenly felt herself being wrenched to one side.

Clarissa was seizing the Duke's arm with fingers like claws digging into his evening coat. "What a silly mistake, Lady Falconer," she cried shrilly, "*I* am his affianced bride."

The Duke looked at her with something like loathing. "You are standing in the way of my fiancée," he said brutally, extricating himself from her grasp. He stretched his hand out to Frederica. Clarissa was bundled unceremoniously away by two large dowagers who kept shaking their turbanned heads over the scandalous lack of breeding in the younger generation. Clarissa was so mad with rage that she would have returned to the attack had not a stentorian voice announced, "His Royal Highness, the Prince Regent." The band struck up "God Bless The Prince of Wales," as the portly figure wearing the Order of The Garter descended the stairs. With the ease of long social practice, the company had formed themselves into two long reception lines in order of importance.

At the very bottom was Clarissa. At the very top was her stepsister. His Highness was laughing and clapping the Duke on the back and chucking Frederica under the chin. Clarissa writhed in misery. But His Royal Highness would surely notice *her*. As yet, her great beauty had not gone unmarked. But the bluff Prince went no further than the beginning of the line and then retired to the card room followed by his cronies.

Clarissa's bitter cup was full. She longed to murder Frederica. Murder her . . . but see her disgraced first. Hard glances were being directed at her as loud murmurs of "What do you expect from the mushroom class," assailed her burning ears.

"Control your fury. You'll win no battles that way," said an amused voice at her elbow. Clarissa swung round. The Honorable Jack Ferrand was standing smiling at her. He was a square-built, soberly-dressed young man with a pleasant, open expression in his light blue eyes.

"We have not been introduced," snapped Clarissa fanning herself vigorously with her ostrich feather fan.

"Come now," he said, not in the least put out, "our paths run together, yours and mine. You wish revenge and I, my dear . . . er . . . wish for revenge as well."

Clarissa, who had started to move away, stopped still. "You are talking fustian, sir," she said, yawning, "but do proceed."

"Come sit beside me behind this wilting palm," he said, "and I will elaborate."

Beginning to be intrigued and anxious to escape from public view, Clarissa complied.

He began without preamble. "The title of Duke of Westerland should have been mine. I am of more noble birth than *Captain* Wright and just as close to the title in line of descent. For reasons that I do not wish to bore you with at the moment, I do not wish that marriage to prosper."

"What will you do?" asked Clarissa eagerly. "Stop the marriage from taking place? Arrange some accident?"

"What a bloodthirsty and vindictive girl you are," he said matter-of-factly. "No, nothing so dramatic.

"I am merely anxious that the marriage should be so unhappy that your sister would remain childless, if you take my meaning."

"And what satisfaction do you get out of it?" demanded Clarissa. "Even if they had no children, you cannot inherit unless the Duke dies."

"I shall get the same satisfaction as you . . . revenge," he said bluntly. "The other reasons are my own affair."

Clarissa blinked her beautiful eyes and stared at the reflection of her feet in the polished floor. This seemingly amiable and correct young man exuded a strange menace. But the longing to see the Duke and Frederica humiliated was too much for her.

"What can I do?" she asked suddenly.

"Leave it to me," he rejoined with a smile of satisfaction. "I will tell you when the time comes how to play your part. The lawyers told me that under the terms of the will,

Westerland must be married within the month. Therefore, I should think the so-happy couple are not in love."

"Of course not," spluttered Clarissa. "Why, only last week he proposed to *me* and was rejected. I . . . left him on his knees and he was *crying* and . . ."

He interrupted her rudely. "If we are to deal together, there must be no lies between us. I have some small acquaintanceship with the Duke and, for all I wish him harm, I know he is the last man to cry over anything, even rejection by such a diamond of the first water as yourself."

Clarissa looked at him sulkily. "Well, he was not exactly crying, but he *did* propose."

"Splendid," said Mr. Ferrand. "We progress amazingly. Now, for the moment, go back and congratulate your young sister as prettily as you can."

Clarissa stared at him, "I confess I do not understand how I became involved in this conversation in the first place. . . ."

"To harm your victim you must first get close to him . . . or her." He leaned forward and stared into her eyes with a peculiar intensity that was almost hypnotic. "Now, you will do exactly what I say."

Clarissa was suddenly frightened. She did not know what on earth she was doing discussing insane plans of revenge with a virtual stranger. With a mental wrench, she turned her face from his and rose to leave. Only a few feet away from her was Frederica on the arm of her Duke. She was laughing at something he had said and gazing up adoringly into his face. Clarissa found that she was trembling with rage and jealousy. Not pausing for any further thought, she tripped forward lightly and flung her arms round the surprised Frederica.

"Darling Frederica, I am *so* pleased for you but it is the *gentleman* who is to be congratulated. Am I not right, Your Grace?" Her beautiful face was alight with happiness and good humor. His Grace found it almost impossible to imagine that this was the girl who had rejected his offer so vindictively. He looked at her in some surprise and Frederica, with some trepidation.

"You must let me help you choose your bride's clothes," she prattled on to Frederica. Clarissa was suddenly conscious of the approving stares of several of the immediate guests and became positively radiant. She chattered lightly and easily and then departed after giving her stepsister a farewell hug. Over Frederica's little shoulder, Clarissa looked across into the eyes of Mr. Jack Ferrand. As he gave a slow nod of approval Clarissa experienced a slight shiver of fear that she had committed herself to some game even more dangerous than the ruin of Frederica's marriage.

The carriage rattled over the cobbles on the road back to Hartford Street. Emily sat opposite Frederica, slumped ungracefully against the squabs, the dashing young lady of the earlier evening having been undoubtedly transformed back into a pumpkin. Emily had been in high alt at the unexpected attention paid to her — particularly by Lord Hefford. But Lord Hefford had unaccountably neglected her towards the end of the evening to pay court to that upstart, Clarissa Sayers.

For once unaware of her new friend's distress, Frederica chattered happily about the ball until she noticed her fiancée stifling a yawn. He smiled his apologies at her. "I'm afraid I wasn't listening to you, Frederica. God, I'm tired. What a curst dull evening!"

Poor Frederica. The glittering evening of her engagement, her gown and jewels, her meeting with the Prince Regent — all shattered like fragile glass and lay in ruins at her feet.

In the darkness of the carriage, she surreptitiously wiped away a tear. In all her excitement and joy of the evening, she had forgotten that, to the Duke, it was just a tedious legal move to be endured to secure his fortune. She became as miserable and silent as Emily and it was a sorry pair of damsels who trailed into the Cholmley home.

Since the Cholmleys rarely entertained, the small drawing room with its spindly, shabby furniture always smelled of damp and disuse. The bulbous eyes of the Cholmley ancestors, who all appeared to have suffered from goitre, seemed to follow Frederica as she walked slowly into the room, goggling and damning this miserable product of the mushroom middle-class.

"I'll leave you two," said Emily abruptly. "Not as if you need a chaperone now you're engaged." With that she strode from the room, her long, mannish strides at odds with the remains of her new-found elegance.

The Duke looked thoughtfully at his fiancée. She was staring down into the empty fireplace with her face turned away from him. He felt suddenly at a loss as to what to say. Perhaps she was already worrying about the more intimate side of marriage. He had better set her mind at ease.

"Frederica," he began, addressing her unresponsive back, "we have not had time until now to discuss our marriage. I wish to assure you that I will keep to the idea of this marriage of convenience at all times. You may have your friends and amusements and I promise not to interfere."

She still remained with her face turned away from him so after a moment's hesitation he went on. "I planned that we should spend our honeymoon at Chartsay which will be our country home. You shall have your own apartments of course." He felt as if he were putting it badly, but goaded by her lack of response continued with, "You shall not be troubled by me *in any way*. In our peculiar situation, it is not necessary that we . . . er . . . we be intimate as man and wife."

Frederica had been so delighted in her new freedom at escaping from Mrs. Sayers that she had thought life would go on like a story book. Henry would fall in love with her, the marriage bells would ring and life would stretch out in one long happy road. She realized with an odd maturity that nothing she could do would force this man to fall in love with her. She could only behave lightly and happily and hope somehow that the miracle would happen.

She forced a smile on her face and turned round. "How *serious* you are, Henry. *I* am not worried about the terms of our marriage. I am only a little tired." But Frederica could not resist just a little dig. "Getting engaged seems to be an everyday affair for you. Curst dull, you called it, if I remember rightly."

His thin face flushed under his tan. "I did not mean that, Frederica. We are friends, are we not? I would as lief be married to you as to any other girl in London. There!"

This was said in a gentle, affectionate voice, and with that Frederica had to be content and cease dreaming that one day his eyes would burn with the fire and passion that they once held when he looked on Clarissa.

Chapter Five

"I really fail to understand you, Mrs. Sayers," said Mrs. Byles-Bondish. "Apart from a singular outburst of hysterics over Frederica's wedding which, by the way, was a resounding social success, you no longer seem to care a rap for her."

Mrs. Sayers sulkily jabbed her needle into a tired piece of petit point and did not deign to answer.

"Further," pursued Mrs. Byles-Bondish, "I find it odd that when the girl ran away from home, however much it was glossed over by Mrs. Cholmley's belated invitation, you did not turn a hair or call in the Runners."

"She is an odd child," snapped Mrs. Sayers. "When we were in Harrogate, she was always escaping from the house. I am well rid of her."

Mrs. Byles-Bondish shook her head in amazement and appealed to Clarissa who had just come into the room after driving with the Honorable Jack Ferrand. "Dear child! Do speak to your obstinate mother.

She will have nothing to do with Frederica and as Duchess of Westerland the girl holds a powerful social position which could be of inestimable value to *you*."

"I do not need help to attract suitors," said Clarissa.

"That I grant you," said her mentor. "But with the exception of Mr. Ferrand, your suitors are not exactly of the first stare. The Marquis of Blandhaven has a doubtful reputation to say the least. The Westerlands will be entertaining at Chartsay. It is of the first importance that you invite yourselves for a visit."

"Toady to that chit? Never!" declared Mrs. Sayers.

Mrs. Byles-Bondish smiled thinly. "I should also conceal your very unnatural feeling toward Frederica," she advised.

Clarissa unexpectedly came to her aid. "I declare I miss my little sister," she said in a sweet voice. "Do let us go to Chartsay, mama. They say it is prodigious grand. Would you not like to stay in an abbey?" she wheedled.

Her voice oozed charm but Mrs. Sayers heard the hint of steel in her daughter's voice. To refuse would be to endure one of Clarissa's famous tantrums.

"Oh, very well," she said, giving in with bad grace.

Mrs. Byles-Bondish smoothed down her serviceable walking dress and tucked an errant strand of grey hair under her feathered bonnet. Her long nose quivered in distaste as she surveyed the loud stripes of the drawing room. She, for one, had every intention of cultivating the new Duchess. She wondered fleetingly how Frederica would fare in the magnificence of Chartsay. Then, with a feeling of relief, she left the Sayers' mansion.

She would not have been very surprised to know that at that moment Frederica was feeling completely bewildered and that she had a feeling that her husband was overawed by the first sight of Chartsay as well.

The old abbey had been redesigned and rebuilt in the eighteenth century by James Wyatt, an architect who favored the gothic style. It looked for all the world like a huge sprawling castle with its multitude of towers and battlements in mellow Portland stone.

To Frederica's bewildered eyes, the park seemed as large as a whole country. She had never felt so small or insignificant in all her life.

All the staff, from the Groom of the Chambers down to the small knife boy, were lined up in the great hall to greet them.

Steward, wine butler, under butler, house-keeper, bakers, housemaids, footmen, coachmen, porters, and odd men all bowed and curtsyed to the newly-married couple. There must be about a hundred, thought Frederica, and *that* was not counting the forty gardeners and forty roadsmen.

The Groom of the Chambers was so awful and magnificent that she felt at one point that he must be the old Duke himself and that the whole affair was a mad farce. His name was Mr. Jeremiah Lawton. Tricked out in livery adorned with so much gold braid, he would have outshone an Admiral of the Fleet, he punctuated all his remarks with a resounding thump of his tall cane. By the end of the introductions he had disdainfully managed to convey by his attitude that he considered the new Duke and Duchess mere upstarts and interlopers in *his* house. He was fat and white like a species of insolent slug and his sister Rebecca, who acted as housekeeper, was no better.

The steward, a middle-aged man called Benjamin Dubble, appeared mercifully pleasant and open-mannered. He begged a few words in private with the Duke who was about to suggest that Frederica retire to her rooms and make herself comfortable when the Groom of Chambers, Mr. Lawton, said in a high, pompous voice that Mrs. Lawton, the housekeeper, would take Her Grace on a tour to familiarize her with the workings of Chartsay.

Frederica opened her mouth to protest that she was too tired but her husband looked pleased and nodded his approval.

Tired though she was, Frederica soon realized that Mrs. Lawton was deliberately making her tour of Chartsay as confusing and as long as possible. Nothing was left unvisited from the bedrooms to the laundry room. She spoke in accents of stultifying gentility and ignored Frederica's every hint that her lecture should be cut short.

On the ground floor, almost the whole of the main block was occupied by living rooms. There was a dining room, drawing room and library, all on a scale suitable for a house which was likely to fill its thirty or so guest bedrooms with house parties. There was also a small billiard room and breakfast room. A huge conservatory led west from the dining room to the chapel, concealing the equally enormous servants' wing from the garden. The north-west wing was a family one into which they could retire for privacy or when the house was empty. Frederica's bedroom was next to her sitting room and had long French windows opening onto the terrace where several aristocratic peacocks screamed all night long as if their necks were being wrung. The Duke's dressing room was across the corridor from Frederica's apartments and opened into a large study.

Frederica's courage fell before the grandeur of it all. She felt like a provincial imposter but parried all Mrs. Lawton's delicate probings as to her background and how long she had known the Duke. From the various portraits on the wall and from the old-fashioned toys in the nursery, she was able to conjure up a different picture of Chartsay, one crowded with guests and the noisy laughter of children instead of all this stiff and formal elegance, glittering and waxed as if encased in glass.

"It looks like a museum!" she burst out.

"But then," replied the housekeeper inspecting her keys, "Your Grace has not been used to anything in *this* style before."

Frederica knew this to be an unpardonable piece of impertinence but she was tired and had not the courage to rebuke the older woman.

At last she was set free to enjoy the solitude of her apartments.

The long curtains of her sitting room moved gently in the summer breeze. She crossed to the long windows and passed through them onto the terrace. Huge urns of roses decorated the stone balustrade. A hazy golden light swam over the long green lawns making the woods in the distance shimmer and dance. She took a deep breath of the clean country air scented with mown grass and roses and felt her optimism returning.

The park was dotted with temples, obelisks, seats, pagodas, rotundas, reflecting pools and two ornamental lakes, each with its fishing pavilion strategically placed on an island in the middle.

Frederica experienced the beginnings of a feeling of pride. All this was hers to share with her husband. She had a longing to see the gardens and park thronged with happy faces and the formal elegance of the rooms warmed by dancing and music. She was so carried away with this vision that she swung round to meet her husband who was coming along the terrace and threw her arms around him. This was noticed by the steward's room boy who told the third footman who told the under butler and from there it moved upwards to the august ears of the Groom of the Chambers who sniffed and inferred that he expected nothing better from that class of person.

"Henry, Henry," Frederica was crying.

"*Do* let us have a drum."

He ruffled her curls absent-mindedly and a frown creased his forehead. "I must say it would be a splendid idea. But I am having difficulty with Lawton. All he seems to do is thump that cane of his on the floor and tell me that the old Duke would never have done this and the old Duke would never have done that. All, mark you, with an undertone of veiled insolence.

"I do not want to offend the old servants with any unheaval but . . . dash it all. There's a whole army of them. They could cope with a royal visit let alone a drum! But I will consult Dubble, the steward.

"But first, we must prepare for dinner, my dear."

"How old-fashioned," exclaimed Frederica. "It is only three o'clock."

"The old Duke," said Henry, imitating Lawton's mincing, high-pitched voice, "*always* had breakfast at nine-thirty, dinner at four and supper at ten, *Your* Grace. So there! And here am I, lord of all I survey, agreeing meekly to dinner at four when I am not even hungry. Well . . . we shall start our innovations tomorrow. Dinner, by the way, is in the state dining room because . . ."

"The *old* Duke always took his meals there," giggled Frederica.

He gave her a quick hug. "Get dressed quickly and we shall face the horrible Groom of the Chambers together!"

Three quarters of an hour later, their Graces faced each other down the enormous length of a dining table laden with plate. They were attended by Lawton, the butler, the under butler and eight footmen. For most of the long and heavy meal, Frederica kept her eyes on her plate, raising them occasionally to look nervously at her husband. Frederica had never imagined such a thing as an almost tangible atmosphere of insolence . . . but there it was. All the staff were correct as to looks and manners, but they showed their disdain in infinitessimal ways — an eyebrow raised a millimeter, a slight twitch of the lips. "It is almost," she thought, "as if they are waiting for me to eat peas with my knife!"

At last the long meal was over and the Groom of the Chambers drew back Frederica's chair to conduct her to the drawing room and so leave His Grace in solitary splendour to enjoy his porte.

An icy hush fell over the room as the Duke seized the decanter and two glasses *with his own hands* and said cheerfully to his wife, "We need not stand on ceremony tonight . . . particularly on our first night here. I shall join you."

They walked arm and arm through the disapproving silence, through the anteroom and into the drawing room where Lawton gave his cane a final thump on the floor and left.

The Duke looked like thunder. "I was a fool! Damned jackanapes. In future, when we are alone, we shall take dinner in my study at seven. Furthermore, you shall have your drum. The local county will be calling tomorrow to pay their respects. Invite who you will and as many as you like.

"They must learn that *we* are in command here. You must get used to issuing orders as well, my dear."

Frederica was too timid to tell him that the very idea of ordering Mrs. Lawton about terrified her.

He stretched one slippered foot towards the empty fireplace and shivered. "We need a good blaze here to warm us. What a vast place this is!" A sea of blue carpet seemed to stretch on into infinity. Various Westerlands stared down at them in the gloom from their gilded frames. Small islands of tables and chairs were grouped at various points in the large room. The Duke tugged the bell and told the answering footman to "make up the fire."

"An' please Your Grace," he said, "the old Duke . . ." and then cowered before the blaze of wrath on Henry's face.

"Light the fire, man," hissed the Duke, "or lose your employ."

"Certainly, Your Grace, of course, Your Grace . . . this very minute, Your Grace . . . I will bring the wood directly . . ." and he Your Graced himself rapidly out of the room.

But both knew somehow that the battle was not over. In the distance, they could hear the Groom of the Chambers approaching, his cane punctuating every step.

Lawton finally stood in the doorway, his eyes popping in his fat, white face. "I hasten to inform you, Your Grace, that the old Duke gave orders that no fire was to be lighted between March and September."

The Duke got to his feet. His icy voice carried to every corner of the room. "Bring the staff here immediately. Every man Jack of 'em. Hop to it, man, and stop puffing and gobbling or by God you'll feel my riding crop about your fat shoulders. And bring candles. Must we sit in this hellish blackness? Get a move on!" The last sentence was shouted full strength and the white-faced Lawton positively ran from the room, trailing his cane behind him like a fat bulldog with its tail between its legs.

First candles were brought until the room was ablaze with light. Then there soon was a fire roaring up the chimney. Then the staff began to file into the room, sidling along the wall farthest from the angry Duke. "Is that all?" he finally barked.

"Yes, Your Grace," said Lawton, "except of course for certain of the outside staff."

"Very well," said Henry. "Now look here the lot of you. And listen hard. Should I have to repeat any of this, you will *all* be dismissed.

"I do not give a damn what the old Duke did or did not do. I am the Duke of Westerland and you will obey my commands. Furthermore, simply obeying my commands is not enough. Any man or woman who betrays the slightest sign of dumb insolence in my presence will be first horse-whipped, then dismissed. Do I make myself clear?"

The Groom of the Chambers swelled out his chest like a bullfrog. "Of course, Your Grace. Of Course!" One of his gold buttons popped off and flew across the floor. He looked so discomfitted and ridiculous that Henrietta let out a nervous giggle. Lawton stooped to retrieve his button. For a split second his eyes met Frederica's and she recoiled from the venom and dislike mirrored there. Then he was immediately polite and obsequious. Everything should be as His Grace desired.

His Grace cut his effusions brutally short and told him to remove himself and his staff immediately.

When they were gone, Frederica stared at her husband, her eyes shining with admiration. "Oh, Henry, you were marvellous!" she cried.

He shrugged. "I'd as lief face several battalions of Boney's troops than cope with encroaching servants. Have a glass of port with me, Frederica. It is not a very romantic homecoming for a young girl but perhaps if you have a few balls and parties, we can contrive to be merry."

But Frederica did not feel very merry when he left her at the door of her bedchamber explaining that he had had a truckle bed set up in his dressing room. She sat up in the great canopied bed in her room feeling very small and alone. Her lady's maid, Benson, had been triumphant over the Duke's "putting these uppity servants in their place" but Frederica could only remember the look of venom Lawton had cast at her and knew instinctively that the Groom of the Chambers blamed her alone for his humiliation. Like most cowardly bullies, he would instinctively select the weaker of the two as a target for his revenge. She remembered the first few days of their honeymoon, spent in the vast grandeur of their town house. The servants had been courteous and polite, but Frederica had been left alone a great deal since her husband was often away on business for most of the day.

She wondered sadly if her husband was thinking about her or if he had fallen comfortably asleep. He had seemed so handsome and brave this evening, mused poor Frederica. Would she always have to be content to be treated as a sort of younger sister?

"No, *never!*" she thought vehemently. Tomorrow was a brand-new day in which to try for his love. Nothing would come in her way.

Their wedding had not turned out the wedding of her dreams. A distant relative of Mrs. Cholmley had been persuaded to give her away. He was a thin, effeminate, elderly gentleman, called Sir Edward Cole, who took it upon himself to disapprove of the marriage from the day of his arrival in London. The bride was too young, he said. He had gone on to cite innumerable instances of disastrous marriages which had taken place between "school girls and rakehelly gentlemen." This jeremiad had continued even as he led her to the altar of St. George's, Hanover Square.

Then her wedding gown had been Aunt Matilda's choice, and Frederica was too grateful to her for her hospitality to protest that it was uncomfortable. Of heavy white silk worn over a stiffened cambric petticoat, it was so encrusted with pearls and silver embroidery that Frederica was frightened that she would fall down under the sheer weight of it. A heavy train of priceless Valencienne's lace was anchored to her small head, making it ache.

The only precious moment of the wedding was when the Duke had turned to watch her coming up the aisle and his handsome face lit up with a warm smile of appreciation. Aunt Matilda had said she looked like a fairy princess and the Duke had appeared to think so as well.

Frederica made her responses in a clear voice which she felt belonged to someone else. When she reached "I do" she became aware that the hysterical sobbing of some female among the guests was reaching a crescendo. The Duke bent to kiss the bride and the sobbing woman gave voice. It was none other than Mrs. Sayers. In a broad Yorkshire accent, she gabbled out against the wicked

Fates who had chosen to make Frederica a Duchess instead of Clarissa. Fortunately her accent was so strong and her voice so choked with sobs that most of her remarks were unintelligible.

Frederica had walked down the aisle in an agony of embarrassment, seeing the faces of the congregation as a blur, hearing the tumbling clamor of the bells, and feeling as if she were holding the arm of a stranger.

But the trials of this evening, she felt, had brought them closer together. And tomorrow, they would be alone.

And with that comforting thought, she fell soundly asleep.

As she tripped lightly into the breakfast room attired in her best pink sprigged muslin with the deep flounces and little puffed sleeves, she found the Duke frowning over a letter. He gave her a distracted smile and threw the parchment down on the table. "This is an express from Mrs. Sayers," he said bluntly. "She and Clarissa are to pay us a visit. In fact, I gather from this that they are already on their road. They have made sure that we shall have no opportunity to refuse them. They are being accompanied by Jack Ferrand, who is a decent enough fellow and related to me in some obscure way. It is, however, a damnable nuisance. There is too much to get acquainted with here and" . . . he hesitated . . . "we have not really had a chance to get acquainted ourselves." He gave her a smile of peculiar sweetness and Frederica's heart turned over.

If only she had the courage to tell this new husband that the last people in the world that she wanted to see were Mrs. Sayers and Clarissa. Would she never escape from Clarissa's icy, biting remarks and Mrs. Sayers' venom? The Duke looked at her distressed face and read her thoughts.

He said, "We will have to have them some time, you know and we may as well get it over now. Once this 'courtesy' visit is over, I shall make sure that they are not invited again. There! Does that please you?"

She nodded dumbly but — oh! — *how* she wished she could bar the gates to Chartsay. The thought of seeing Clarissa again in the company of her husband made her feel positively ill.

That breakfast seemed later to Frederica to be the last time they were to be alone together. No sooner had they finished than the local county came to call in droves. Then, when he was not receiving guests, the Duke was closeted in his steward's room, dealing with problems of the estate from the repairs to cottage roofs to what to plant in the five-acre field.

Faces came and went during the day, each visitor fortunately calling only for the regulation ten minutes. Curious faces, high-nosed faces, degenerate faces, inbred faces went in and out of the drawing room in a seemingly endless stream.

The arrival of the Rector, Dr. Witherspoon, and his plump comfortable wife was the only pleasant interlude in the long day. Mrs. Witherspoon was comfortably if unfashionably dressed in a round gown of cambric and a poke bonnet with several drooping osprey feathers. Her cheerful, rosy-cheeked face with its shrewd little eyes seemed to register the uncomfortable atmosphere created by the now-fawning servants and the faint smell of disuse which hung about the enormous room. Seeing that the Duke was relaxing in the Rector's company, Frederica suddenly confided to Mrs. Witherspoon that she felt sure that there could be nobody left in the whole county to call and suggested a walk in the grounds.

Mrs. Witherspoon gladly assented and walked with Frederica out into the golden sunshine of the afternoon.

Frederica was not yet acquainted with the grounds but she suggested they should walk to a rotunda by the edge of one of the ornamental lakes. They moved slowly across the grass companionably discussing gowns and recipes.

"It is a fine and handsome home you have, Your Grace," said Mrs. Witherspoon at last, plumping her stout figure down on a stone bench in the rotunda.

"I' faith, it is indeed," said Frederica sadly, looking across at the great sprawling pile. "I am not used to such grandeur."

"There, there," said Mrs. Witherspoon, patting her hand. "You will soon become accustomed to it, I dare say. And then you have always me at the rectory to run to, my dear. We have a snug place, rather shabby I admit, but it suits me very well. We are only a short ride from Chartsay, you know.

"Is Lawton behaving himself?" she asked abruptly. Frederica hesitated and then confessed that they had experienced a certain amount of trouble on their arrival.

Mrs. Witherspoon nodded her head in satisfaction. "That one had too much of his own way when the old Duke was alive. The old man was a bit of recluse, never saw a soul or gave so much as a breakfast party so Lawton and that army of servants ran things pretty much as they pleased. The way Lawton went on you would think that Chartsay was his. You would be well advised to get rid of him *and* that precious sister of his."

"But they have been here so long," pleaded Frederica, feeling cowardly. She told Mrs. Witherspoon of her husband's confrontation with the servants.

"Bravo!" she cried, clapping her plump hands together. "But mark my words, it's easy for the men, particularly a man like His Grace who's used to commanding a battalion. If you have any trouble, just come to me."

Frederica felt very comforted. They strolled back across the lawns in companionable silence.

After saying her goodbyes, something made Mrs. Witherspoon turn in the doorway and look back. Frederica stood alone in front of the double-arcaded carved screens at the back of the great hall. In the shadows of the staircase which rose up almost to the high-vaulted timber ceiling ninety feet above she glimpsed the fat white face of Lawton. He was watching Frederica rather as a large fat cat watches the linnet in his wicker cage. Mrs. Witherspoon gave a shiver and made a half-step to go back until she became aware of her husband tugging at her arm. "What is the matter, Mrs. Witherspoon," teased the rector. "Did someone just walk over your grave?"

"No," said Mrs. Witherspoon slowly. "Not mine."

Chapter Six

Frederica dressed with especial care for dinner. It was to be served in the Duke's study and they would be alone — apart from the usual retinue of servants.

She tried not to feel disappointed when she opened the door of the book-lined study to find that the Duke had invited his steward, Benjamin Dubble. Both men were concerned in carrying on their earlier discussions of repairs and harvests so that only Frederica noticed Lawton's eyes bulging with jealousy because of the steward's favored treatment. The old Duke, thought Frederica sourly, would *never* have done such a thing!

But the Duke had noticed her sad face and put it down to the exhausting day of visitors. When the meal was finished and Frederica rose to her feet to leave the men to their wine, her husband unexpectedly proposed that they do without it. He would take Frederica for a walk on the terrace instead.

Mr. Dubble's romantic heart was touched. He rose with profuse apologies.

He had forgotten they were newly-weds and an old man like himself would not play gooseberry. He looked at them both with such affection that Frederica's heart began to lighten. Life at Chartsay might prove to be pleasant after all, despite the fact that Mrs. Lawton had tried to bully her earlier over the matter of the dinner menu.

The air on the terrace was cool and pleasant as they strolled along. A faint light above the trees was all that was left of the dying day and a splendid moon turned the glassy water of the lakes to beaten silver.

Frederica stole a look at her husband's profile in the moonlight. He seemed very formal, grand and remote in his faultless evening dress of black coat and knee breeches, his profile framed by the high starched points of his cravat. Then he turned and smiled down at her and said, "Alone at last . . . to coin a cliche. Oh hell!"

Frederica started in surprise and followed his gaze down the long driveway. A dusty traveling chariot pulled by four steaming horses was bowling up the drive, the lozenge on its side lit by the flaring torches carried by the outriders.

"Mrs. Sayers!" he said. "I had begun to hope that she had changed her mind and did not plan to come."

With her heart sinking down to her little slippers Frederica made to walk from the terrace but he held her back. "Let them receive the full Lawton treatment. We can meet with them after they have been shown their rooms. No doubt Mrs. Sayers will tell Lawton exactly what she thinks of his old Duke this and old Duke that and it will serve both of them right!"

Mrs. Sayers in fact did just that and before she had reached her rooms. "I do not care what the old Duke did or did not do," she remarked, poking Lawton in the back with her umbrella. "My son-in-law is the Duke here now and if he has not impressed that upon you already, I will make it my business to see that he does!"

Again, in the way of all bullies, Lawton retreated before this formidable opposition and decided to concentrate his energies on Frederica. It was all *her* fault that she had such an obnoxious and vulgar mother!

While their guests removed the stains of travel, Frederica and her husband repaired to the drawing room where Jack Ferrand was the first to arrive.

He was attired in his usual modest dress and his pleasant face beamed with delight on the married couple. Frederica was just beginning to relax in his easy and undemanding company when her mother and Clarissa were announced.

Frederica had all but forgotten her stepsister's beauty and even the Duke felt a slight constriction at his throat as she sailed into the room and enveloped Frederica in waving, gauzy, palest-pink Indian muslin. She then prettily begged for permission to kiss her new brother-in-law, wrapping her white-gloved arms languorously round his neck as she did so and making poor Frederica feel like a gawky schoolgirl.

Had she not been so upset, she would have found the change in her stepmother ludicrous. Mrs. Sayers was all languid condescension to the new Duke — she had obviously found a new model to hide her tough north country soul behind. Her coy simpering, her quite awful flirtatious onslaughts on the Duke, sat at odds with her plump, tight-laced figure and heavy jaw.

"I must apologize for not calling on you at your own house," began Mrs. Sayers. "But I believe young married people should be left alone." She let out a sudden shriek of laughter and rapped the Duke painfully across the knuckles with the ivory sticks of her fan. "Rude man! I declare I know *exactly* what you are thinking." The Duke opened his mouth to protest but Mrs. Sayers, fortifying herself with champagne, was in full flight.

"But when my sweet Clarissa says to me, 'Mama, I am faint with worry over my darling sister,' I realized my duty — so here we are!" She looked appreciatively around the room. "Very elegant! A fitting setting." Her small eyes, resting briefly and adoringly on Clarissa, left the other three in no doubt as to whom the setting was perfect for. "Heppelwhite!" she then exclaimed in satisfaction and, having solved the origins of her chair, turned her full attention on her stepdaughter. "Frederica, I gather you are to hold a drum," said Mrs. Sayers. "Very proper. It is right that Clarissa should become acquainted with the local county. I told that housekeeper, Mrs. Lawton, I told her right to her face, 'My little Frederica may not be in the way of knowing how to go about holding grand parties but with the help of her mama, she will contrive admirably.' " Frederica closed her eyes and prayed to God her mother would disappear, but when she opened them Mrs. Sayers was still beaming with smug satisfaction and her husband was engrossed in conversation with Clarissa. She could not hear what they were saying because they were seated a distance away, but she saw Clarissa laugh and blush and the smile on her husband's face made her wish she were dead.

Mr. Jack Ferrand hitched his chair closer to Frederica. "You are looking uncommonly well, Your Grace." She smiled and thanked him, glad of the diversion. "I hope we are not intruding on your private life." He gave her a sudden sympathetic grin. "Your mama was determined to come and you know how it is, once she has an idea in her mind, there's no stopping her. But let us discuss your party. Do you plan to have many people?"

Frederica answered him with enthusiasm, liking his open face and easy manner. Yes, she intended to ask most of the county. The house was large enough, goodness knows. Mr. Ferrand edged his chair even closer. Had she considered a masquerade? It was all the crack. Of course, there was nothing *fast* about it. The guests unmasked before midnight. But then, Mrs. Sayers would probably not approve. "This is my home and I shall do as I please," remarked Frederica with some heat. "My love," she addressed her husband who looked up in surprise at the unexpected endearment. "I have decided we will have a masquerade."

"For our first entertainment?" he exclaimed in some surprise. "Very well, my dear. As you wish."

Mrs. Sayers opened her mouth to protest but encountered a long, cool look from Clarissa and closed it again. Frederica blinked a little of her triumph and it was some few moments before she realized that she did not really want to have a masquerade party after all.

Frederica had hoped for a few words in private with her husband before they retired for the night but the visitors followed them as far as their rooms, sticking close to the newly-weds with the tenacity of cupping glasses.

As she closed her door, Frederica heard Clarissa trill, "Oh, Henry, did I tell you of the latest *on-dit?*" Her voice dropped to a seductive murmur and Frederica stood rigid, her tiny hands clenched into fists. To go back and join them as they lingered in the corridor seemed over-possessive. Ignoring the questioning look from her maid, she allowed herself to be undressed and went to bed with one pleasant thought among the other troubled and nasty ones — that Jack Ferrand at least seemed an unexceptionable young man.

The Duke kept early hours for breakfast so she was at least sure of his company for part of the morning. But her face dropped miserably as she entered the breakfast room on the following morning to find Mrs. Sayers, Clarissa and Jack Ferrand already there and making plans for the day. It was with no little relief that she heard her husband explain that he would have to leave them to their own devices that afternoon as he meant to drive Frederica to call on the tenants. He gave his wife his singularly sweet and heart-twisting smile and she smiled back, their eyes meeting and holding each other's gaze for a second. Jack Ferrand caught the exchange of looks.

He said, "If you can spare your wife this morning, Duke, I should appreciate her escort round the grounds."

The Duke readily agreed and said in that case he would, for his part, show Clarissa and her mother round the house. Frederica noticed Clarissa's radiant smile of assent and only hoped that Mrs. Sayers would not plead the headache as she often did when she wished to allow Clarissa ample freedom to demonstrate her charms.

Jack Ferrand turned out to be a cheerful and amusing companion, exclaiming with wonder and appreciation at the wide vistas and smooth lawns. Innocent Frederica did not realize that each chatty remark was carefully planned to drip poison into her heart. Jack Ferrand teased her about her marriage. She knew of course that her husband had been labelled as a rakehell and a heart-breaker, he said with such a happy laugh that Frederica felt she could not possibly be so missish as to take offence, especially when he gallantly added that it was obvious that Frederica had indeed captured the Duke's fickle heart. And, he added, she must not be annoyed by all the malicious gossip that the Duke had married on the rebound. People were simply jealous. Poor Frederica! She had not been long enough out in the world to know that gentlemen did not talk with young matrons with such freedom. Her eyes began to mist over with tears and she desperately cast her eyes around the grounds for some-thing to point to in order to change this heart-breaking conversation.

"What is that door built into the hillside?" she asked, pointing with the ivory end of her parasol to a sturdy embossed door beside the lake.

"How intriguing!" cried Jack Ferrand. "Let us explore."

Frederica hesitated. "Have we time? The sun is high in the sky and we do not want to be late. I wouldn't want Harry to leave on his rounds without me."

"Now, how could he possibly leave such a pretty bride?" teased Jack Ferrand. He grasped the handle of the door and gave it an energetic pull. It swung smoothly open, showing a long, low cavernous passage. A candle and tinderbox were placed on a ledge at the entrance which he lit, sending mysterious shadows dancing up the low brick walls. Then he paused. "Wait a bit. I think I hear someone calling. Go ahead and explore and I will be back directly."

Frederica picked up the candle and moved slowly down the corridor. The air became chillier and chillier and she began to shiver. The passage ended in a great vault piled high with glistening blocks of ice and straw. Ice! She was in an ice house. She remembered tales of such places as these on country estates where the blocks of ice were drawn from the lake in winter and stored in the depths of the vault to supply ice for the great houses in summer.

She held her candle high above her head noticing long stalactite forms hanging from the roof. Suddenly these grew masses of red eyes blinking in the wavering candlelight and Frederica heard the slow rasping sound of leathery wings. Bats! She gave a faint scream and turned about. The daylight at the end of the corridor seemed very far away and just as she made towards it, the door slammed closed with a tremendous bang. The disturbed bats wheeled and squeaked and she crouched down on the floor of the corridor, wondering if she would faint from fright.

The Duke's barouche was waiting outside the abbey, the horses pawing at the gravelled drive. The Duke paced up and down the steps and then turned to question Jack Ferrand for what seemed to be the hundredth time. "And you say you have no idea of where my wife might be?"

Jack Ferrand shook his head. "We were strolling in the grounds and I went off a little way because I thought I heard someone calling and when I came back, she had gone."

Clarissa fluttered out on to the steps, carrying her bonnet and parasol. "Could you take me instead, dear Henry?" she begged. "Mama has gone to sleep and it is such a beautiful afternoon."

The Duke hesitated. He was very angry with Frederica. She should have realized how important this visit was to the tenants. He was still distrustful of Clarissa but she looked so enchanting and so guileless that he decided to let her come with him.

The barouche swung down the drive under the long line of elms and Jack Ferrand watched it until it was out of sight. He thought momentarily of Frederica imprisoned in the ice house and shrugged. He would let her out at the precise time when he judged the Duke to be still angry and not yet worried.

Frederica crouched on the floor of her ice prison and shivered uncontrollably from cold and fright. She pressed herself against the outer door, hearing the faint sounds of summer filtering through as if from another world. She dared not move for fear of arousing the sleeping bats. She began to wonder about Jack Ferrand. Had he deliberately shut her in here? But why? Perhaps the door had simply swung shut and he had assumed that she had left. But her husband would surely not leave without her. That was the only comforting thought she had, but even that began to fade as the long afternoon wore on and gradually the faint light from the crack under the door grew dimmer. "He will come. Oh, please God make him come," prayed Frederica. As if in mocking reply, the candle gave a final spurt and went out. Then the slow, sinister rustling of the bats began again.

Frederica began to cry hopelessly. Her husband did not even care enough to have the grounds searched. She had heard no voices calling, no sounds of hurrying feet.

Suddenly, almost noiselessly, the door of the ice house swung open to reveal the moonlight shining on the lake. With legs that could barely carry her, she pulled herself up from the floor and staggered outside. There was no one there, nothing but the sound of wildfowl rustling in the reeds and the occasional plop of a leaping fish.

Wearily she dragged herself across the lawns and towards the great house. The long drawing room windows were ablaze with lights. Moved by a sudden impulse, Frederica mounted the wide stone steps to the terrace and looked inside.

Her husband was standing on the hearthrug talking to Clarissa while Jack Ferrand and Mrs. Sayers lounged in opposite chairs and indulgently looked on. Diamonds sparkled on Clarissa's white bosom and at her ears, and winked from the intricate embroidery of her high bodice. On a lesser beauty, the effect would have been ostentatious and vulgar, but Clarissa looked magnificent. She was laughing at something the Duke said and playfully reached up her hands to straighten his cravat.

He did not care! She had been missing nearly all day and he did not care! With her heart like lead, Frederica trailed along the terrace and entered her bedroom by way of the French windows. She had neither the heart nor the courage to join the party. Without summoning her maid, she slowly undressed and crawled into bed, listening with anguish to the faraway sounds of laughter from the drawing room.

After what seemed an age, she heard her bedroom door being gently opened. The face of her husband seemed to swim above her in the flickering candlelight. "Well, my lady wife," he said grimly, "next time you have the headache and choose to retire to your room for the day, please inform me in time. It was well that your stepsister offered to act for you, and to my relief, she behaved very prettily. The tenants were charmed."

All Frederica's misery fled before a wave of suffocating fury.

"For your information, I have spent the most hideous day of my life locked in the ice house."

He looked at her skeptically. "And who let you out?"

Frederica faltered, "The door simply swung open on its own accord."

"Then why did you not come to the

drawing room to let me know of your safe return?" he demanded in a cynical voice.

Frederica bit her lip. How could she tell him of her watching them from the terrace? How could she tell him of her heartache?

"I will tell you what *I* think happened," he said grimly. "You could not be bothered to visit our tenants and stayed away until I had left. You became angry because Clarissa had gone instead of you so you decided to stay in your rooms and sulk like the child you are!"

Before she quite knew what had happened, Frederica had picked up the pillow from behind her head and thrown it straight in her husband's face.

"How dare you!" she screamed. "I spent horrid long hours, frightened out of my wits, half frozen to death and all you cared about was flirting with Clarissa."

He straightened his cravat and remarked unforgivably, "You are a jealous little cat!"

Never in her much-bullied life had Frederica been so angry. She flew from her bed to her dressing table and began to hurl everything and anything she could get her hands on at her equally-furious husband who slowly edged his way towards her despite an onslaught of pins, lotions, scents, and curling tongs.

He seized her by the wrists and twisted her arms behind her back staring down into her infuriated face. "I have a good mind to give you the thrashing you deserve," he said grimly, glaring down at her. "As my wife, you will have to learn how to behave. *As my wife!*"

A wicked gleam began to appear in his eyes and he forced her backwards toward the bed. "I know of one very good way to school you, Miss Frederica." He bent his head and his firm, cool lips clamped down ruthlessly over her own. Then raising his head and looking down at her with a dawning surprise, he deftly picked her up and threw her on the bed and before she could move, hurled himself on top of her, driving the breath from her body. He caught her flailing arms and pinned them behind her and bent his head again, forcing her back into the pillows with long, slow insulting kisses. As she tried to free her hands he dug his nails into her wrists. She let out a long scream of pain. Immediately he rolled off her and reached for the candle. "You are hurt," he said anxiously holding up the light. She mutely held up her battered, bruised and bleeding hands. "Did I do that?" he asked in a whisper.

She shook her head and said in a shaking

voice, "It was the ice house door. I . . . I hurt them pounding on the ice house door."

"Oh, my dear," he said. "Tell me very slowly what happened."

In a faltering voice, she related her walk in the grounds with Jack Ferrand, telling him how the ice house door had mysteriously closed and then opened again in the evening.

"I cannot understand this," he said, shaking his head in bewilderment. "Oh, I believe you, my dear. Do you think Ferrand locked you in? He told me some story that he thought he had heard someone calling and went to investigate and when he returned, you had gone."

"He did go to investigate," said Frederica, "but did he not mention anything about the ice house?"

The Duke shook his head. "Then I began to wonder aloud where you might be and Clarissa said that one of the servants had mentioned that the Duchess had retired to her rooms suffering from the headache and did not wish to be disturbed."

"But none of the servants saw me . . ." Frederica began.

"Don't trouble your mind about it at this moment," said the Duke, gently interrupting her. "I shall get someone to bandage your hands and then I would like to have a few words with Mr. Ferrand." He reached his hand toward the bell pull and then hesitated. "I owe you an apology, Frederica. I am afraid I have a devil of a temper."

She gave a shaky laugh. "I have just discovered that I have one myself." She began to giggle helplessly. "You . . . you do *smell* so. I must have thrown a whole bottle of scent over you."

He wrinkled his nose. "The whole room smells like a Covent Garden brothel."

Frederica looked at him wearily, all the laughter gone from her face. "And how, my lord Duke," she demanded coldly, "do you know how a Covent Garden brothel smells?"

He ruffled her curls. "Keep your claws in, my kitten. It is just an expression, nothing more. And one that I should not use in front of any lady. Please forgive me."

He smiled into her eyes and Frederica thought that when he smiled like that she could forgive him anything.

He pulled the bell and gave her a sudden quick kiss on the cheek as the maid came hurrying into the room. He left Benson exclaiming in horror over the damage to her mistress's hands and went in search of Jack Ferrand. He found him alone in the small billiard room, and in the split second before Mr. Ferrand leapt to his feet, the Duke had an uneasy feeling that his visit was not unexpected.

"Your Grace!" cried Jack boyishly. "This is damn fine claret your old relative laid down. Care for a glass?" The Duke shook his head and leaned his broad shoulders against the mantleshelf and surveyed his guest. Jack Ferrand's light blue eyes looked ingenuously up into the Duke's. He radiated friendliness and good humor. The Duke took him step by step through his walk with Frederica and then stopped him when he described their arriving at the ice house. Jack Ferrand clapped his hand to his brow. How *could* he have forgotten to mention the ice house? But he had heard someone calling, he *had* returned, and seeing the door closed, assumed Her Grace had left. Good God! It made him sick to think of it.

Watching his face closely, the Duke noticed that it had indeed gone very white and strained. He realized he had misjudged his guest and forgave him for his error of omission. He would have to look elsewhere for the culprit. With a courteous bow His Grace left the billiard room . . . and Jack Ferrand with his hands shaking.

For his face had indeed gone white during

111

the Duke's interrogation but not with fear for Frederica. It was because the Duke, looking down at him from his great height, and icily putting his questions with that damned haughty drawl of his, had looked every inch a Duke. And Ferrand's jealousy burned so deep, he thought he might die from it. He poured himself another glass of claret and drank it with a gulp. By the time he had finished the decanter, hope had risen anew. Such a guileless pair as the new Duke and Duchess could be easily duped. One only had to find the right time and the right place. Of course he hadn't meant to kill the girl, but only to scare her and give Clarissa a chance to ingratiate herself with the Duke. Although, Lord knows, murdering Frederica would be easier than trapping a rabbit.

But next morning, after he was roused by the commotion in the great hall below, and had hurriedly dressed to see what was afoot, he no longer felt so sure of the vulnerability of Frederica.

It was an almost medieval scene which met his eyes as he emerged onto the first landing of the great staircase. The lights from the arched mullioned windows shone down on the servants assembled below. Clarissa and Mrs. Sayers were standing open-mouthed at the entrance to the breakfast room. The Duke stood half way up the stairs facing his staff.

He raised an imperious hand and the assembly shuffled into silence. "My wife was locked in the ice house yesterday," declared the Duke. "I am unable to find the culprit but mark my words . . . my wife has to be guarded from harm at any hour of the day. Should any harm befall her like the happening of yesterday, the heads of the household staff will be instantly dismissed. That is all."

The servants scurried off. Clarissa looked up and saw Jack Ferrand looking down at her and she turned hurriedly away.

Despite her dislike for Frederica, she suddenly found the news that the girl was to be guarded at all times immeasurably comforting.

The Duke had questioned her closely about her story that Frederica had retired with a headache. Which servant was it? Man or woman? Could she identify the servant?

Clarissa had taken refuge in rudeness. Stifling a yawn, she had said that, really, all the servants looked alike to her and if her *dear* brother-in-law bombarded her with any more questions, why, she declared she would have a bad case of the headache herself!

Chapter Seven

It lacked but two days to the great event of Frederica's masquerade and already the great house was abustle with preparations.

Emily and Mrs. Cholmley, complete with her holy interpreter in the form of Stafford, had arrived, much to Frederica's delight. At first Emily had been sulky and despondent, declaring the masquerade party to be a great bore, but the arrival of Lord Archie Hefford put an end to her moping and she became as frantically interested in the subject of costumes as any other lady there.

Everyone was overcome with the desire to surprise the others and kept the subject of his costume a closely-guarded secret.

Frederica had seen little of her husband since the night of her escape from the ice house. He had taken hurried meals in his study and then spent the days riding over his land with his steward, seemingly immersed in the intricacies of agriculture. For once, Frederica had surprisingly little difficulty in arranging the great evening's menu with Mrs. Lawton. She did not know that Mrs.

Lawton feared that if she did not comply with Her Grace's wishes, then Her Grace's formidable and vulgar mother would be down on her like a ton of bricks.

She and her brother went about their duties with a false air of calm and willing obedience and only Frederica was not deceived. She had heard Mrs. Lawton whispering to her brother that "one day, *she* will be on her own here and then we'll get our revenge."

Frederica had shuddered and determined never to live at Chartsay without the escort of her strong husband. She was in no doubt that she was the "she" referred to so viciously. She had mentioned the overheard conversation to her husband at a moment when he was busy and pressed for time. He had accused her rather abruptly of being over-sensitive and pointed out if she were to take up the habit of eavesdropping, she would be in for a lot of nasty surprises. Then he had ridden off before she could protest.

She could only be glad that her husband had even less time for Clarissa than for herself, although Clarissa seemed to make the best of her few moments, always smiling, always beautiful, and always hinting at some secret intimacy with her large expressive eyes.

But Clarissa was privately wearying of the

game — especially since the arrival of Archie Hefford. She also felt caged by Jack Ferrand's perpetual stage-managing and when he informed her that the Duke was going dressed as Sir Walter Raleigh, and that she should therefore go as Queen Elizabeth, she had yawned and said vaguely, "Oh, very well."

Her little stepsister, Clarissa was beginning to realize, could be quite charming company — although decidedly naive. Look at the way she kept working on that great horse of an Emily who was breaking her heart over Archie Hefford.

Jack Ferrand was not very worried over Clarissa's apparent lack of interest in revenge. All it needed, he knew, with people of Clarissa's nature, was some small slight, some prick to their vanity, to bring the wrong side uppermost. He would wait until an opportunity arose.

Little Frederica danced through the great halls, checking on the needs of her guests, and cheerfully made plans for Emily's happiness. Her sister-in-law, she decided, should go as Cleopatra. With a black wig, and a little stain on her face to darken her skin, Frederica was sure she would look magnificent. Mrs. Sayers overheard her idea and related it to Clarissa. "Pon rep!" cried

Mrs. Sayers, wiping her streaming eyes, "Can you imagine that great maypole of a girl as the Queen of the Nile?"

Clarissa gave a cat-like smile. "And wait until the great maypole hears of my betrothal to Archie Hefford."

"Indeed!" cried her mother. "At last, my child. When did he propose?"

"He didn't," said Clarissa, adding with languid assurance, "but he will. I shall be the most beautiful girl present, shall I not?"

"Yes, my dear," said her mama dutifully.

But it was not a simple little prick to her vanity that Clarissa was to experience on the night of the ball — it was a series of full-scale humiliations.

At the start, she felt that her Queen Elizabeth costume was too cumbersome and her hair scraped under the high Tudor cap was hardly becoming. She was about to remove it and wear an ordinary ballgown but then she thought, since she would be such a perfect foil for the Duke, that she would be taken to be the Duchess by many who had not yet met Frederica. And Clarissa had enough malice left in her heart to enjoy that prospect.

In order to make an effective appearance, she kept to her rooms until the last minute before descending the staircase to join the reception line into the ballroom. Almost the first person she saw was the Duke, shaking hands with his guests. To her horror, he had changed his mind and elected to wear modern evening dress, a glittering mask his only concession to the masquerade. The diminutive and exquisite figure of the little Spanish princess stood beside him and, through eyes misted with jealousy, Clarissa realized that her little stepsister had surpassed herself. Frederica was dressed in a black lace crinoline which accentuated her tiny waist and creamy bosom. Her midnight black hair which had never been cut to the modern fashion was piled high on her head and confined by an ebony comb and a black lace mantilla.

Queen Elizabeth in her massive Tudor gown, her face rigid with anger under her awe-inspiring cap, found herself in danger of being a wallflower for the first time in her life. The gentlemen took one look at that forbidding figure and began to court less terrifying-looking ladies. By the time Clarissa had fled to her room, beaten her maid, reduced the hairdresser to tears and torn every ballgown out of her closet until she could find something suitable, over an hour had passed. When she finally descended, looking her usual exquisite self, she had regained some of her former good humor. Several gentlemen who had sworn to favor the card room and not dance at all, suddenly changed their minds at her appearance and she was again courted and feted in the manner she was accustomed to. She was determined to have her revenge on Jack Ferrand for suggesting such a ridiculous costume when the music abruptly stopped.

The Duke mounted to the musicians' gallery and held up his hands for silence. "It gives me great pleasure," he cried, "to announce the engagement of my dear sister, Emily, to my very dear friend, Archie Hefford!" He smiled and waved his hands towards the long windows where the couple was standing outside on the terrace. Everyone applauded and Clarissa turned slowly. Could that be Emily? Good, old, plain, dull Emily? She was a real figure in her gold and black Egyptian robe with a long silky black wig and a high gold helmet. Her face was transfigured with happiness and love.

Clarissa's heart burned with black hate. The glittering throng applauded and cheered, their masked faces glittering in the candlelight, seeming to Clarissa like so many mocking demons. She had been so sure of Archie Hefford. So sure! Someone would pay for this, and dearly. She turned and saw Jack Ferrand watching her with a malicious gleam in his usually pleasant eyes. "Come into the grounds, sir," she hissed. "I would have a reckoning with you!"

"But of course, dear lady," he said smoothly, offering her his arm. Clarissa walked in a seething silence, almost dragging her companion along with her until they reached the rotunda where Frederica had once sat with Mrs. Witherspoon.

Clarissa rounded on him, her eyes blazing. "Now Ferrand . . ." she began, and then broke off. He had drawn a pistol from the pocket of his highwayman's costume and it was pointing straight at her heart.

"Take off your clothes, Clarissa," he demanded.

She turned white with anger and fear. "I will do no such thing. Are you mad?"

By way of an answer, he pressed the gun against her ribs.

Tears of pure rage and fright began to roll down Clarissa's cheeks. "No!" she cried, backing away from him. "Why do you do this to me, sir? Have I not helped you enough? My mother will. . . ."

He gave her a jeering laugh. "That old upstart can't do much for you when you are lying lifeless. I repeat . . . take off your clothes. You do not do as I say, and I shall shoot you dead. It will be assumed that some prowler killed you in the grounds. I have alibi enough, I assure you!"

Clarissa looked into his pitiless eyes and realized she had no other choice. Turning her back to him, she fumbled with the fastenings to her dress and with trembling fingers let it fall to the ground at her feet. The moonlight illuminated the rotunda with a soft radiance, showing him Clarissa's trembling back. She was wearing the latest thing in scanty petticoats and pale pink silk stockings delicately embroidered with silver thread, rolled below the knee.

His cold light eyes raked over her body. "Just as I had hoped," he said at last. "That is quite a disfiguring birthmark you have on your left thigh."

Clarissa felt the blush starting at the soles of her feet and rising to the top of her head. To think she had overcome her mother's protests against the new flimsy, transparent petticoats!

Jack Ferrand's voice was heavy with menace. "Now, listen to me, my girl. You will do what I say or I will tell the world and his wife that I have lain with you. I will be able to describe the little mole there . . . and there . . . and of course the birthmark. Your

121

mother will not dare deny it. You will be labelled Haymarket ware, my dear, and never will you win your title. Now, you will entice the Duke into some compromising situation so that his little wife thinks him unfaithful. I will then persuade the hurt couple to return to London where it will be easier to keep them apart. Tell anyone of this evening and I will kill you. Put on your clothes."

Clarissa looked at him wide-eyed. "You are not going to rape me then?" He walked round the shivering girl and surveyed her insolently from head to toe.

"Rape! *You*," he laughed. "Good God, it would turn my stomach." And still laughing, he turned and left her.

After he had gone, Clarissa slowly put on her clothes. Her very brain seemed to be warped and twisted with hate. First she would indeed revenge herself on Frederica. Had it not been for Frederica, she could have married the Duke. Had Frederica not interfered, then she could have married Archie Hefford. And after she was finished with Frederica and married to some rich lord and did not have to account for her expenses as she had to at the moment with such a prying mama, she would pay and pay dearly to get Jack Ferrand removed from the face of the earth.

She glided quietly into the ballroom and was soon surrounded by the group of admirers. Over their shoulders she saw the Duke dancing with his wife. He was smiling tenderly down at her. There was no time to be lost.

The Duke was at that moment remembering the feel of Frederica's body underneath his on the bed that night they had had their quarrel and was making up his mind that it would be pleasant to repeat the experience . . . but in a more tranquil atmosphere. Everytime she looked into his eyes, Frederica's heart sang with joy. They paused at the edge of the dance floor when the music ceased, pleased with their home, and suddenly very happy in each other's company. Clarissa came dancing up and some of Frederica's happiness spilled over as Clarissa pouted prettily and said her dance card was half empty because she had looked such a quiz as Queen Elizabeth.

"Oh, Henry will dance with you," cried Frederica, giving Clarissa an impulsive hug. "It is the waltz and you know how you love to waltz!"

Clarissa moved readily into the Duke's arms and, after giving them one indulgent look, Frederica went to sit beside Mrs. Cholmley.

As the dance led them near the windows, Clarissa saw Jack Ferrand watching her and shivered. "You are cold!" exclaimed the Duke. "Let us go away from the windows."

"No, indeed, I am warm enough," said Clarissa, "but I am in very great trouble and I need your advice. Could you step onto the terrace with me? Just for a moment."

The heavy curtains had been drawn against the night air and the Duke hesitated a moment, doubtful of the propriety of the suggested move. But Clarissa's beautiful eyes were bright with unshed tears and she indeed seemed to be in trouble. He pulled back the curtains and ushered her out onto the terrace.

"How can I aid you, Miss Sayers?" he asked politely. She gave a breathless little laugh. "Oh, call me Clarissa. We are related now, you know." This was received with a stiff bow so she hurried on. "I am in such deep trouble. Mr. Ferrand has proposed to me and I do not know whether to accept or not."

"That is surely a matter for your heart to decide."

She moved closer to him. "But my heart is already engaged." A perfect tear rolled down her cheek. "When you proposed to me, I wanted . . . oh so much . . . to say yes. But mama made me refuse. That is why

I was so cruel. I do not care for titles or for any other man."

He made a half turn to leave. "I find this conversation distasteful," he said coldly. "Also, it is insulting to my wife."

"I know I am behaving badly," breathed Clarissa. "But I am so jealous of her." This indeed held all the ring of truth. "I feel that I should settle for a conventional marriage. There, you see! I have decided to be sensible. I shall accept Mr. Ferrand perhaps."

"Really, Clarissa," protested the Duke. "What is it you want of me?"

"Just one kiss of farewell," she said sadly. "Is it so much to ask?"

He looked at her doubtfully. "I suppose not. Now, if I kiss you, will you go back to the ballroom and try to forget all this nonsense."

"Oh yes," she sighed, winding her arms around his neck.

"See how closely they cling together," whispered Jack Ferrand in Frederica's ear. He had drawn the curtain a little way to reveal the Duke with Clarissa in his arms. He had waltzed her away from Mrs. Cholmley and across the dance floor after Clarissa and the Duke, praying that his timing would be right.

He was almost disappointed when

Frederica neither went out on the terrace to make a scene or fled from the ballroom. With two burning spots of color on her cheeks, she returned to her guests and chatted and laughed in a high brittle voice until the evening finally came to an end and she could put her aching heart to bed and relieve her feelings in a bout of tears. Only Emily noticed that something was wrong and, had Frederica confided in her, then her troubles would have been at an end. For Emily was a forthright girl and would have challenged her brother on the spot. But Frederica wearily remembered that she had embarked on a marriage of convenience. She had no right to storm or rage at her husband.

She gave a shudder as she saw Jack Ferrand approaching with his usual charming smile. "My dear Duchess," he whispered. "I am much distressed. It was surely a fleeting moment of weakness on the Duke's part. After all. . . ."

"We do not discuss our private affairs," said Frederica icily. "Be so good as to take your hand from our arm."

Jack Ferrand raged inwardly. Damn her for her sneering ways. She should be heartbroken. He swallowed his venom and went on smoothly as if she had not spoken.

"London is of course a whirl of delights at this time of year," he said smoothly. "You must miss it."

Frederica presented him with one black lace shoulder and began to talk to Mrs. Cholmley who called on her butler Stafford for translation. But the idea of London was already burning into Frederica's brain. In London, she could make friends of her own, and be constantly absent from home, attending everything from Venetian breakfasts to turtle dinners. London should swallow her up, complete with her broken heart.

She smiled and curtsied to the departing guests, never once looking in her husband's direction. She escaped nimbly to her room as soon as the last guest's carriage had rumbled down the drive.

She stood as stiff as a wax doll while Benson undressed her, and then tumbled headlong into bed and buried her aching head beneath the pillows. She heard her husband's light step in the corridor outside and then she heard him enter her sitting room. With a gasp, she flung herself from the bed and locked her door. A minute later, she heard him try the lock. If he had called to her, pleaded with her or said he loved her, she would have swallowed her pride and unlocked the door. But he only remained for a second outside and then she heard him slowly going away to his rooms on the other side of the corridor.

Well, she would declare her intention of returning to London in the morning. And . . . and . . . he could stay here with all these horrid servants for all she cared. She would be happy and popular and . . . and . . . be all the crack and have lots of beaux. And she would show her handsome husband that she did not care a jot.

And with that comforting thought, she put her head down on the pillow and cried herself to sleep.

Chapter Eight

The Westerland home in Grosvenor Square — if such a modest word as home could apply to the palatial town house — soon saw the Duke and Duchess back in residence.

The Duke had complied with his wife's request because he had business in town and hoped that the social air would revive his young bride's moping spirits. Yet he now found himself left alone too much with Clarissa for comfort as Frederica seemed to have a genius at absenting herself at all times of the day.

Unlike Chartsay, the town house had remained fairly untouched since the eighteenth century, boasting pastel tinted walls in the vast reception rooms and flock wallpaper in the private apartments. The carved staircase was a miracle of Grinling Gibbons art and, despite the fact that Mr. Walpole may have damned the classical fireplace as "little miscarriages into total Ionic," Frederica felt more at home than in the splendor of Chartsay. Her bedroom reflected the Chinese vogue of the middle of the eighteenth century, having a splendid gold and black lacquered bed with a canopy of writhing scarlet dragons.

The old Duke had kept a completely separate staff at the Grosvenor Square residence, and the difference between it and the one in the country seemed to Frederica incredible. Under the iron rule of a well-trained butler, they were quick, deferential and polite. At the beginning, she had determined to assert herself by making changes on the daily menus presented to her. But these were received by the housekeeper with such smiling goodwill that she eventually left the army of servants to run things themselves since they seemed able to cope efficiently whether she interfered or not. Emily had helped her with a quick survey of the housekeeping accounts and, though the bills seemed horrifying to the as-yet unsophisticated Frederica, Emily assured her that they were quite the thing. She was not being taken advantage of in any way.

The new dashing Emily also suggested that she might modernize the house in the Duke's absence, but to Frederica modern meant Mrs. Sayers' passion for noisy and vulgar stripes. She preferred to retain the faded eighteenth-century elegance of her home.

The downstairs salon, mostly used for visitors, was the only modern room, being decorated in the current Egyptian mode with black and gold borders of sphinxes on the walls and sphinxes' heads staring from the pilasters of the fireplace.

Frederica had plunged into an orgy of spending, buying greens and golds and crimsons for her wardrobe since she did not have to wear the unflattering pastels considered suitable for a debutante. Her circle of acquaintances grew and she became a familiar figure at the opera or in the park.

The Duke planned an expedition to Scotland to view his estates in the north. He naturally expected Frederica to go with him and was surprised when she announced her intention to remain in London. Where, he wondered grimly, was the shy miss who once took every opportunity to be alone with him? He was confronted instead by a dashing young matron who traced patterns in the carpet with the ivory tip of her parasol and refused to meet his eyes when she reminded him that theirs was a marriage of convenience. He felt hurt and angry but had to agree with her since he had clearly set the terms himself. He accordingly departed on his lonely journey for the north, unaware that as soon as his carriage had disappeared from view, his young bride cried as if her heart would break.

Frederica finally dried her eyes and could only be glad that her husband was far removed from Clarissa. Her stepsister had become a constant visitor and Frederica could not refuse her company. And every time Frederica took precedence far above her at a ball or assembly, Clarissa became more determined than ever to carry out Jack Ferrand's wishes despite the hold he had over her.

Never by word or look had he referred to the dreadful night of the masquerade but his calm assumption that she should be ready to receive him at all hours of the day told of his power enough.

After the Duke had been absent for a month, Jack Ferrand made one of his abrupt calls on Clarissa. She came down the stairs tranquilly enough to meet him. There was little he could expect her to do with the Duke gone from town. And she had already set up some very promising flirtations which she wished to see mature undisturbed. Her heart sank as she entered the drawing room to find him pacing restlessly up and down. He whirled around as she came in and began without preamble. "Something must be done before Westerland returns," he snapped. "Your dear sister has snubbed me on occasion after occasion and last night was enough! I solicited her hand for a dance at the Jennington's ball and she said meekly that she had the headache and did not care to dance and the next minute I saw her waltzing off in the arms of that superannuated old fool, Giles Bellamy."

"You have only yourself to blame," remarked Clarissa spitefully. "You could not help gloating over her when she saw me and Henry together."

He stopped his angry pacing. "I thought that would have been enough to break the marriage. But now I have another weapon for us to use."

"Us?" questioned Clarissa faintly.

"You, rather, since your dear sister will not let me near her. There is a French *emigré* I know, of devastating charm and looks. He is low both in funds and in moral fibre — just what we need. He is plain Monsieur Duchesne but we shall rename him Le Comte Duchesne and furnish him with the necessary funds to keep up his appearance."

"I don't understand. . . ." began Clarissa but he interrupted her rudely.

"You never do, my hen-witted friend. The Comte is to lay siege to Frederica's heart. She cannot love the Duke. You are sure there was no scene following the mas-querade?"

"For the hundredth time NO," snapped Clarissa. "She was very quiet, of course, but nothing out of the way."

She looked up at him suddenly. "What have *I* to do with this so-called Comte? My part is simply to flirt with Henry which I can't do at the moment."

"You dull-witted jade," he roared. "Frederica will not let me near her and would be suspicious of any friend of mine. The Comte shall escort you to the opera to-night and you will take him to your sister's box. He will take things from there. But be careful! Archie Hefford is back in town and I don't want him putting a spoke in our wheel."

When he took his leave after some final in-structions, Clarissa moved to the window and watched him crossing the square. She had a sudden longing to tell everything to the Duke on his return, but the thought of the consequences made her shudder.

Unaware of the dark plans that were cir-cling around her head, Frederica wearily prepared for the opera that evening.

She found herself sometimes day-dreaming of Chartsay — a Chartsay without the Lawtons, a Chartsay filled with friends like the rector and his wife, friends one could be comfortable with for an evening instead of the constant straining conversation to be endured nightly with a host of new acquaintances. There would not be much consolation in the music tonight, she reflected. The opera was a place to see and be seen. The constant shuffling movement from box to box went on even during the performance. The top ten thousand were not happy unless they were all crushed shoulder to shoulder in some small suffocating place. With an expertise beyond her years, Frederica had learned to avoid the over-familiar overtures of some of her determined gallants.

Clarissa would no doubt be there, fluttering her eyelashes and telling the world how she doted on her little sister, and Mrs. Sayers would be waving her plump and mottled arms as she described the glories of Chartsay to her twittering circle of toadies. And Mrs. Byles-Bondish would be stage-managing in the background attired in some costly gown, the bill for which would be somewhere in Frederica's desk.

Shortly after her return to town, Frederica had received a call from Mrs. Byles-Bondish. That stately if withered lady had announced to the startled Duchess that she had bespoke a new wardrobe and had requested that the bills be sent to Frederica. "For you know, my dear Duchess, as I am one of your family so to speak, you would not wish me to continue to appear as a dowd." This effrontery was delivered in such a calm, well-bred manner that she had gone from the house before Frederica had even begun to think how she should cope with the situation.

She shuddered to think what her normally open-handed husband would say about it on his return, but her thoughts quickly returned to the present when the arrival of her escort for the evening was announced. With a little sigh she picked up her fan and prepared to descend the stairs.

Her escort for the evening had been carefully chosen. A young and languid Dandy by the name of Peregrine Pellington-James, he professed a passion for Frederica which was as false as his head of golden curls. Frederica had become the fashion in a small way and Mr. Pellington-James was merely following the fashion.

Though he flirted boldly in public, he was almost inarticulately shy in private and patently grateful to Frederica for allowing him to cut a dash in front of his friends.

He was a sturdy plump young man with a broad, rosy, countrified face which he hid behind a mask of white lead. He was as corsetted and beribboned and scented as Mrs. Sayers but managed to achieve the air of a bluff country squire unwillingly performing in a masquerade.

He swept Frederica a magnificent leg as she entered the room but the intricate whalebone in his corsets locked and he slowly keeled over on the carpet in front of her. Unabashed and trying not to giggle, Frederica rang the bell and summoned the aid of two burly footmen to straighten the distressed young man out, retiring tactfully to the corner of the room while they wrestled under his waistcoat and finally freed the interlocked stays with a snap like a pistol shot.

"And how do you do this evening?" asked Frederica politely when he had been stood upright again.

"Very well, I thankee," said Mr. Pellington-James, waving a gossamer wisp of handkerchief and releasing a little yellow cloud of scent, strong enough to stun a cockroach at forty paces. "Is there any news of your husband?"

"I believe he is shortly to return," lied Frederica. She did not want him to know how feverishly she searched the mail every morning, crying with disappointment each time not so much as a line arrived from the north.

They experienced some difficulty as they settled themselves in the carriage. Mr. Pellington-James proved to be so tightly laced that he could not sit down. Cushions were produced from the house and he lay back against them, staring up at the quilted roof of the coach. No woman could suffer more for beauty, reflected Frederica.

There was more difficulty when they arrived at the opera house. Two footmen had to push and pull the large gentleman out of the coach and then heave him upright in the forecourt of the theater. Puffing and panting, he shook out the lace at his wrists, seized his long be-ribboned cane in one hand and then offered Frederica his arm with a great flourish. But as they swept towards the entrance, Frederica felt a wrench at her arm which nearly overset her. To her horror her large companion went hurtling off backwards into the crowd. His long cane had stuck firmly between two cobbles and catapulted him out of view into a mass of grinning Hogarthian faces. The servants moved like lightning and in no time at all Mr. Pellington-James had been plucked from the crowd. But he was in a sorry mess. His lace had gone from his throat and wrists, along with his diamond stick pin. His shoes were minus buckles and his wig was on sideways.

"So sorry," he gasped. "My dear Duchess, do proceed into the opera. I shall join you later after I have changed. Here, fellow!" he snapped his chubby fingers.

"Escort Her Grace to her box," he commanded one of the footmen. "Apologies. Sincere apologies, dear Duchess." He turned to the crowd. "Murderers! Robbers! *Canaille!*" he yelled.

They cheered back, "Go it, fat 'un. That's a great barrel o'lard ye've got along o' ye, missus!" and various other insults in mercifully too broad a cant for Frederica to understand. The harsh warning rattle of the watch sounded at the end of the street and the crowd dispersed as if by magic.

Feeling shaken and very unprotected, Frederica had a sudden stab of longing for the powerful escort of her husband.

The opera had already begun when she took her seat. Glad that she had not invited any guest other than the unfortunate Mr. Pellington-James, she was able to let the world of society slip away and lose herself thankfully in the music. When the house lights went up she was still caught in the opera's magic spell and focussed dimly on the magnificent entry of the refurbished Mr. Pellington-James into her box. She pulled herself together to cry out desperately, "Oh, please don't!" as he bent over her hand. But it was too late. His treacherous corsets locked again and with the slow, inexorable movement of a vast avalanche, he toppled headlong over the edge of the box and crashed into the pit below.

Frederica stumbled to the door of her box to rush to his aid and ran into the arms of Clarissa and her escort. "Pray be seated, my dear Duchess," said a tall, very handsome man with a faint French accent.

"I will attend to all."

Still she would have followed but Clarissa held her back. Both women peered over the edge of the box.

The handsome Frenchman shortly appeared below, quickly reaching the injured man's side despite scores of angrily shouting men and fainting women. Two attendants appeared and the great body was heaved onto a make-shift stretcher.

Gallant to the last, Mr. Pellington-James raised his eyes to Frederica as he was borne away and kissed his plump, be-ringed hand to her.

Clarissa was unusually solicitous. "My dear Frederica," she cried. "Pray be seated and relax. The Comte will take care of everything." She hesitated for a minute, wondering whether to rush her fences and tell her stepsister that the Comte was vastly enamored of her, but decided against it, knowing that Frederica met all unsubtle approaches with dignified disdain.

The Comte returned to the box just as the house lights were dimming for the second act. Clarissa whispered that they would stay with her in case of further mishap.

But Frederica was no longer able to concentrate on the music. She was aware of a new and powerful personality beside her. She was also aware that the Comte was studying her in the darkness.

When the lights went up for the second time, Frederica was able to see the Comte clearly. He was dressed with tasteful and quiet elegance. His most startling feature was a pair of emerald green eyes, framed by heavy lashes, which glittered oddly in his thin, handsome, white face. His jet black hair, as black as Frederica's own, was dressed in the style known as Windswept — a miracle of the hairdresser's art. When he smiled, his whole face lit up with an irresistible charm. Frederica realized that if she were not so completely in love with her husband, her heart would indeed be in danger.

He was introduced as Le Comte Duchesne and like many French *emigrés* had a sad tale to relate of lost lands, lost fortunes, and degrading flight from the land of his birth.

He then began to tease Frederica gently over the downfall of her escort, establishing a subtle atmosphere of intimacy between them with his laughing eyes and charming smile. He was delightful, he was witty, and he was extraordinarily handsome. Frederica felt very young and breathless, somehow a little of the lonely aching of her heart lessened, and by the end of the evening she heard herself agreeing to ride with the Comte in the park next morning.

It was only when she had left him that she realized with some amusement that the handsome Comte had so bewitched her that she had forgotten to inform him that she hardly knew one end of a horse from the other. But why worry! She had observed many ladies riding staid mounts in the Row.

There was nothing to it, surely, for all that horsy people talked and talked. One simply found a quiet animal from the stables, one sat on top, the animal moved, and that was that.

She did not feel quite so optimistic in the morning despite all the glory of a blue velvet riding dress which had hung unused in the wardrobe since her marriage. It was unfortunate for Frederica that the town servants were so correct, for although the head groom wished to ask Her Grace whether she had ridden before or not, he did not dare for fear of seeming impertinent. He contented himself with selecting the most docile animal from the stables instead. Since there were no suitable mounts for a lady, he chose a large hunter which should have been put out to grass months ago.

Frederica smiled nervously at her companion from what seemed to be an enormous way from the ground. The Comte looked even more handsome than she had remembered in his snowy cravat, black velvet coat and shining hessians. His huge black steed snorted and cantered and pawed the ground and made Frederica's knees shake with terror. To her relief, he set off at a slow walk with Frederica's large hunter following amiably behind.

As they reached the park gates, she began to feel more confident. Very few riders were abroad at that early hour. The grass gleamed like green glass under its coating of dew. A faint breeze moved the leaves of the trees and the hum and bustle of London fell away behind her. A nervous quiver ran through the great beast beneath her as it tossed its head to smell the air of freedom. The head groom had elected to escort her himself and he eyed her hunter with an anxious eye. There was undoubtedly something in the lax way Her Grace held the reins which made him fear that she had had little experience in riding.

"Will you forgive me, Duchess, if I give my mount his head," called the Comte. "He is fresh and restless." And indeed he was, having changed masters over the card table the night before. Frederica waved her hand in assent and the Count galloped off headlong down the path. Before Frederica's groom could grab her bridle, her horse had tossed up its head and followed suit.

Her mouth open in fright to form the scream that never came, Frederica clutched the pommell for dear life as she hurtled past trees and bushes. Finally the horse slowed to a canter and she was thrown helplessly up and down on the sidesaddle. Trees and sky whirled round for a few crazy seconds, then there was a sickening thud and Frederica felt herself lying on the ground, stunned and shaken, but miraculously unhurt.

Hooves thudding, the Comte galloped to

the scene. He sprang from his horse and gathered Frederica in his arms murmuring endearments in French, which Frederica did not understand, Mrs. Sayers having considered any education for females to be an utter waste of money. "There is nothing more charming to a gentleman," she was wont to say, "as a completely uninformed mind."

But something in his tone of voice rang alarm bells somewhere in Frederica's brain and she detached herself from his embrace and struggled dizzily to her feet. Still she could not bring herself to confess that she had never ridden before, and luckily her groom stepped forward, saying that Her Grace was obviously too shaken to remount and that he would ride and fetch the carriage.

The shrewd Comte had sensed her withdrawal and immediately began to chat to her, walking along by her side, until she obviously felt reassured. He must not rush his fences, he decided, if he were to earn his salary from Jack Ferrand. He looked down at her animated little face and felt a slight twinge of misgiving. But to draw back now would mean to return to the hand to mouth existence of picking up what he could at the card tables. Luck had been with him last night and it had amused him to play for the horse instead of money. Thanks to Jack Ferrand's munificence, it was a whim he could afford.

"Move quickly," Jack Ferrand had cautioned, "before people become too curious and some nosy French aristocrat decides to enquire into the lineage of the Comte Duchesne."

He had already asked after the Duke's health and hearing (as he already knew) that he was absent in Scotland, said teasingly that she must miss him. "Yes, very much," Frederica had answered simply.

He sensed a loneliness in the girl and quickly decided his best approach must be that of a friend. This idea was to be reinforced a few minutes later.

A heavy horse came wheezing and panting towards them carrying its equally wheezing and panting burden. Magnificent in a frogged coat complete with gold epaulettes and a curly-brimmed beaver hat came Mr. Pellington-James. Apart from a few purple marks which shone faintly through the white lead on his face, he seemed not to have suffered much from his fall of the night before. He ponderously dismounted, catching his high-heeled boot in the stirrup. He hopped up and down, cursing genteelly,

146

as he tried to free himself while his uncaring horse cropped the grass. There was a terrific rending sound as his canary yellow inexpressibles cracked under the strain. Finally freeing himself, he turned with a much flushed face, keeping his back against his placid mount.

"My dear Duchess!" Chuffy bent his head by way of a bow so as not to reveal too much of his back.

To the Comte's amazement, Frederica did not seem at all embarrassed by the sartorial collapse of her friend, merely exclaiming with relief, "Ah, here is my carriage, my dear Mr. Pellington-James. Allow my coachman to escort you home."

Mr. Pellington-James stuttered his thanks and, clutching the remnants of his dignity about himself, climbed in. As the carriage rumbled off, he asked Frederica rather huffily who the demned Froggie was, waving his hand at the Comte who was riding outside. Frederica explained the little that she knew, and Mr. Pellington-James, eyeing the Comte's slim muscular figure, felt and looked so miserable that it took all Frederica's efforts to restore him to his customary good humor.

"What a quiz of a fellow," remarked the Comte lightly as Frederica's carriage rumbled off with Mr. Pellington-James wheezing and puffing inside and his horse wheezing and puffing outside as it trundled along at the rear, obviously resenting the unaccustomed pace.

Frederica looked at him with a little displeasure and then said coldly, "Mr. Pellington-James is indeed prone to accidents but he is truly a gentleman for all that. And I must be careful in my choice of escorts with my husband gone from home."

"I hope you will consider me a . . . er . . . safe escort, my dear Duchess," he said with his charming smile lighting up his face. "Come, we shall be friends, shall we not? We Frenchmen are *very convenable* . . . conventional . . . you know."

He smiled at her so warmly and openly and he *had* declared the innocence of his intentions. Frederica smiled back. "I shall be glad to be your friend, Monsieur Le Comte."

He took her hand and bent over it, depositing a light kiss on her glove. "Perhaps you would care to drive with me to Richmond tomorrow? I have an open carriage so you will not need any escort."

Frederica shook her head and experienced a little pang of disappointment. "I am engaged to take luncheon with the Jenningtons."

"I shall engage you for another day," he said looking into her eyes. *"Au revoir."*

Frederica tripped lightly into the house, her disastrous attempt at riding completely forgotten. It would be pleasant to have such a charming escort. She thought guiltily of Mr. Pellington-James.

So far, he had been the only gentleman of her acquaintance who was openly glad of her company and who could be relied on to *behave* like a gentleman in any circumstances. But his frequent accidents, although treated lightly by a society used to eccentric behaviour, did embarrass her, and maidenly modesty alone stopped her from begging him to find a new corsetiere.

At times she wished with a longing that was like a physical ache that she had gone to Scotland with her husband. But the memory of the way he had held Clarissa in his arms still hurt. She would not beg or plead for his love. But she could not help wondering if he ever thought of her.

At that precise moment, the Duke was indeed thinking of her. Another day's hard riding and he would be home. He had been hurt and angry when Frederica refused to accompany him on his journey. Now, in a gentler frame of mind after his long absence, he realized that he had never tried to woo his wife. She was his property and he had somehow expected her to fall into his arms. Well, he would begin afresh as soon as he reached Grosvenor Square. Never once did he think that Frederica's affections would stray elsewhere. He knew enough of his bride to know that she was honest and direct. But then, sometimes one fell in love most unsuitably, as he himself had done with Clarissa. The thought that London might be abounding in male versions of Clarissa suddenly made him swear under his breath and spring his horses.

It was as well for his peace of mind that he was unaware that a particular male version of Clarissa in the shape of the Comte was abroad and busily plotting his wife's downfall.

The Comte explained to Jack Ferrand that his plan to take Frederica for a drive had gone awry. She was engaged for luncheon at the Jenningtons.

Jack Ferrand paced the floor of his study. "If we leave matters too long, the Duke will be home. I have it! I shall send our dear Duchess a note supposedly from the Jenningtons cancelling the luncheon. You will appear on the scene at the right moment and renew your offer."

The Comte leaned lazily back in his chair and surveyed Mr. Ferrand. "It amazes me why you wish to ruin such a sweet miss. It is of no concern of mine. I am glad of the money as you know. But my curiosity, my dear sir, gets the better of me from time to time."

"My affairs are no concern of yours," snapped Jack Ferrand, rounding on him angrily. "Do as you are bid or crawl back to your gaming halls to scrape your living."

"So be it," shrugged the Comte. "I shall be off to plan our dear Duchess's ruination. 'Tis a pity she is not more like her sister, Clarissa. Now, that one I would enjoy taking down several pegs."

He strolled off and Jack Ferrand continued to pace up and down and back and forth. His plan must succeed. With Frederica out of the way, he could then turn his mind to getting rid of the Duke, perhaps implicating Frederica in the murder. But first he must remove the possibility of any heirs standing between himself and the Dukedom. He had been so sure of the title. All his life he had studied the family tree, watching one successor drop out after the other. How he managed to overlook Captain Henry was beyond him.

151

He sat down and carefully worded a note and signed it 'Mary Jennington'. Then he rifled through his desk until he found a seal close to the Jennington coat of arms and stamped it down on the hot wax as if it were the Duke of Westerland's neck. He was sure that Frederica would not examine the seal closely.

And she did not. But on the following morning the Comte found an unexpected obstacle to his plans. Mr. Pellington-James was there before him, and amazed at the news of the cancellation of the Jennington's luncheon.

"I saw Lady Jennington last night," he protested, "and she said naught of any change of plan. May I see the letter?"

Comte neatly caught the letter as Frederica was handing it over. "Ah, you are only jealous, Mr. Pellington-James, because you know I wish to take the Duchess driving."

Mr. Pellington-James puffed and disclaimed, still holding out his hand for the letter which was being firmly crumpled in the Comte's long fingers.

"Come, Your Grace," pleaded the Comte. "The sun is shining and we are wasting time. You have never been to Richmond but you *have* been to many luncheons. And I am the most correct of escorts. I have an open carriage so you do not even need your groom. Quickly, now," he added in a teasing voice, "before some less correct admirer snaps you up. I am sure your husband would not like to find you sitting at home moping."

His remark about her husband brought a vivid picture of the Duke together with Clarissa. Her sensitive mouth folded in a firm line. "It will take me a few minutes to fetch my bonnet. Thank you for your invitation, sir."

After she had left the room, the Comte leaned back at his ease, not deigning to make conversation with such an over-dressed fop as Mr. Pellington-James. He was therefore unaware of the unusually shrewd and speculative look in his companion's eyes.

Mr. Pellington-James was just opening his mouth to say something when Frederica tripped into the room. The Comte cast him a mocking glance and then held out his arm to Frederica.

Mr. Pellington-James could do nothing but bend over her hand and wish her a pleasant drive.

Some forty minutes later, the Duke of Westerland strode into the hall and handed his hat and gloves to the butler. "Is Her Grace at home, Worthing?"

The butler shook his head. "Her Grace has gone driving. I heard the gentleman mention Richmond as the destination, Your Grace."

The Duke fumed inwardly. He had childishly hoped to surprise his wife and now he felt a fool for not having warned her of his arrival. "Who is escorting her?" he asked striding across the hall.

"Le Comte Duchesne, Your Grace."

"Never heard of him."

"Your Grace! There is another gentleman in the Egyptian Room. A Mr. Pellington-James."

Good God, thought the Duke. I have arrived back in the nick of time. My wife's admirers seem to be everywhere.

He was confronted by a portly young gentleman who was bent over in a deep bow. To his annoyance, the irritating Mr. Pellington-James continued to bow. Again the Duke bowed back and still Mr. Pellington-James presented only the curly top of his blonde wig.

"Enough, man!" said the Duke testily. "Can I help you in any way? Are you waiting for my wife's return?"

"No!" said Chuffy. "I was just sittin' thinkin'."

The Duke found to his surprise that his hands were trembling with anger. "My dear sir," he said icily, "I would like to know what *you* are doing here with my wife gone from the house?"

"I was worried, you see," said Chuffy sadly. "I was wonderin' and wonderin' about your wife going off with that suspicious lookin' Frenchie and. . . ."

"The Comte! Suspicious? Explain, or do I have to choke it out of you?"

"Now, now," said Mr. Pellington-James soothingly. "Violence won't get you anywhere," he added with a gleam of humor. For all his bulk and dandified dress, Mr. Pellington-James was no coward. He went on to explain about the Jennington's cancellation and how there was something about the Comte he did not trust. He made as if to pick the crumpled letter from the floor but the Duke forestalled him.

"Better let me do that," he said. He straightened out the letter, then turned it over to inspect the seal. "That's not Lady Jennington's seal!" he said as he felt the beginnings of fear in the pit of his stomach.

"There y'are!" cried Mr. Pellington-James triumphantly. "Knewd there was something havey-cavey about the fellow. 'Course, that's the French for you. *Emigrés* be damned. Damned lot of Bonapartist spies if you ask me. Now you was in the Peninsula. Tell me. . . ."

"Mr. Pellington-James," said the Duke in a slow, measured voice. "Strange as it may seem, I am all of a sudden anxious for the safety of my wife. How did she come to meet this popinjay? Think, man. Think!"

The fat gentleman corrugated his brow so that little flakes of lead cracked and fell down onto the shoulders of his green silk jacket. "I've got it! It was at the opera. Miss Sayers introduced us."

"Clarissa! I shall call on her directly. Good day to you, sir."

"Wait a bit," said his companion plaintively. "Can't I come with you?"

The Duke looked at him coldly. "You force me to point out that this is no affair of . . ."

"Well, it is in a way," said Mr. Pellington-James good-naturedly. "I have a great regard for Her Grace. We have a sort of . . . lemme see . . . what did that Greek call it . . . ?"

"Platonic."

"Yes, that's it. Platonic. 'Course," he added chattily, following the Duke into the hallway with a childlike confidence in his welcome, "Her Grace is all the crack and I was no end pleased to be able to cut a dash

156

with her in front of the Tulips. Her Grace likes me, you know," he added simply.

Despite his companion's ridiculous appearance, the Duke was beginning to understand why. The fat man, for all his foppery, radiated honesty.

"Very well, then," he said. "But we must take our horses for speed."

"That's all right," said Mr. Pellington-James. "I've got Pegasus outside. Didn't bring the carriage."

The Duke called for his fastest horse to be brought round and then stood on the steps with his new friend and looked at Pegasus in some dismay.

Pegasus was leaning against a horse trough, fast asleep. Even in his sleep, he wheezed and panted.

Good manners stopped the Duke from insulting any man's horse, even such a broken-winded creature as this. If Mr. Pellington-James could not keep up then he would have to be left behind.

By the time they reached the house in Clarence Square, Mr. Pellington-James and the Duke were on first name terms. The dandy confided that his name was Peregrine, but that all his friends called him Chuffy. He begged His Grace to do the same.

Clarissa was fortunately at home and all fluttering arms and melting eyes to welcome "her dear brother-in-law."

The Duke cut through the courtesies and came to the point. "Who is this mountebank of a Comte you have introduced to Frederica and whereabouts in Richmond have they gone?"

Clarissa's mind worked feverishly. She knew that Frederica had been taken to an inn outside Barnet and not anywhere near Richmond.

The Duke surveyed the silent girl. "I do not like the fact that you have to consider your reply, Clarissa. If anything happens to my wife, then you will be held responsible. And I shall use my new social status to make sure that any blame falls squarely on you."

Clarissa bit her lip. This was something she had not expected. She suddenly hit on a plan to extricate herself and still smear Frederica's character in some way.

"They have gone to Barnet," she said suddenly. "Something was said about visiting a sick aunt of the Comte. But they did not tell me much and I was sworn to secrecy and I thought . . ." She let her voice trail off delicately and hung her beautiful head.

"Thank you," said the Duke through stiff lips. "Come, Chuffy. Let's to Barnet."

He had expected to leave Chuffy Pellington-James far behind, but miraculously the fat, wheezing horse kept up a tremendous pace. Any time that Pegasus looked liked flagging, Mr. Pellington-James whispered something in the animals ragged ear which seemed to spur the old horse to positively Herculean efforts.

"I hope we are still in time," yelled the Duke above the wind as they raced neck and neck through Highgate village scattering geese, chickens, children and dust on either side. Chuffy's heart sank. So the Duke was thinking the same thing — that the aunt did not exist. He took a quick look round at the high hedges and sprawling fields. With any luck, Frederica would realize that she was not on the road to Richmond before it was too late.

But apart from wondering from time to time when she was ever going to see the river Frederica did not guess that they were moving rapidly in the wrong direction. She had practically no knowledge of the countryside surrounding London . . . a fact of which Mr. Ferrand had been well aware.

She was wearing a Dunstable straw bonnet over a laced cap, a black and white striped gingham gown and a white Norwich shawl. The sun flickered through the trees casting rippling shadows over her companion's face.

He had been unusually silent since they left the streets and houses of London behind, devoting his whole attention to his horses. His speed contrasted oddly with the leisurely pace with which they had left Mayfair. The Comte had encouraged Frederica to stop and speak to various of her acquaintances and each time he had laid a large hand possessively on her arm, causing several raised eyebrows. Frederica felt vaguely that it was not at all the thing, but she did not want to refine too much upon it for fear of seeming missish. When she chided her companion for his silence he only answered briefly that he was in a hurry to reach Richmond in time for lunch. Frederica was just about to ask him to slow his pace because she was beginning to feel travel sick with all the lurching and bumping of the country roads, when a village came into view at the top of a steep hill. "Richmond?" she asked hopefully.

He shook his head. He did not want her becoming suspicious because she could not see the river before he had her safely at the inn.

"It is a village before Richmond. We are to stop for lunch just on the other side. You are looking rather pale."

"I am feeling unwell because of the unnecessarily fast pace of this carriage, sir," said Frederica tartly, straightening her bonnet. Her companion did not reply, and the carriage swept through Barnet without slackening pace. They continued out into the windy fields on the other side of the village, where vast clouds of rooks soared and tumbled like so many birds of ill-omen.

"Pray, sir!" cried the Duchess. "When exactly do you mean to stop?"

He had spied the thatched roof of his destination so he promptly slackened the reins and smiled down at her. "We are just arriving. This is a simple country inn, but I can procure you a glass of lemonade." He swung the carriage from the road and up a long, bumpy dirt lane to where the inn lay at the end. With its heavy thatched roof and the sun sliding across its windows as they drew near, Frederica felt as if the inn were slewing its eyes round to peer at her from under a heavy head of straw hair.

She suddenly realized that she was very far from home with a man she knew little of and began to feel a small knot of fear forming in her stomach. The inn looked deserted.

"I have decided I wish to return to

London," she said firmly.

To her surprise, the Comte said mildly, "And so you shall." He deftly turned the carriage until the horses were facing back down the road again.

He jumped down from the carriage and smiled up at her, the wind ruffling his black curls and his green eyes dancing with amusement. "I declare you were beginning to be frightened of me, Duchess," he teased. "Come! Admit it. You were beginning to wonder why this so-strange French Comte is taking you to a small out-of-the-way *auberge*. No?

"Well, the reason I stopped here is because it is but a little way off our road and this unprepossessing hostelry has a charming garden at the back. I discovered it when I was with the Des Leschamps."

Frederica had the grace to blush at her fears. The Des Leschamps were a very high-nosed family of impeccable lineage and terrifying propriety.

She allowed him to help her down from the carriage and together they walked towards the door of the inn. The taproom was low-raftered and sunny but smelled abominably of beer and bad drainage. Frederica wrinkled her little nose and made to retreat. Just then a burly man made his appearance,

162

stooping to enter through a narrow door at the back. He was dressed in a smock-frock, leather chaps and heavy wooden clogs. With his heavy matted hair, low beetling brows and small searching eyes, he looked remarkably like the inn.

"Ah, mine host!" cried the Comte gaily, pulling Frederica forward. "Lead us to your . . . er . . . garden."

"The garden, zur," grinned the yokel, and then winked and giggled and tugged his forelock to such an extent that Frederica thought he was about to have a fit. He pushed open the low door and stood back, grinning and bowing to let Frederica past. She found herself peering into a low-raftered bedroom and, with a cry, tried to draw back. A hearty shove in the small of her back catapulted her into the room and she fell headlong on the floor. The door was slammed behind her and the key turned in the lock.

She heard the chink of money being exchanged in the taproom and then the burly "landlord" demanding in a peeved voice, "Can't un stay ter watch, zur?" This was met by rapid curses in French and the sound of a blow and then the heavy clogs could be heard trudging off in the distance.

Frederica picked herself up off the floor

and ran to the small window. Never opened, it was now warped shut. There was an iron bed in the corner of the room covered with a greasy patchwork blanket and, apart from a hard upright chair, there was no other furniture in the room.

She whirled round at the sound of the key in the lock and found herself facing her captor. Leaning against the door jamb, he looked solemnly down at her frightened face. "I am sorry this happened, Frederica," he said bluntly. "But I am being paid to do this and I need the money."

"Who is paying you?" whispered Frederica, "And what are you going to do?"

"The purpose of this," he said, not meeting her eyes, "is to ruin your reputation. You will stay here with me for the night and I suggest you . . . er . . . lie back and enjoy it, as you crude English put it. Otherwise, you will find the exercise somewhat painful."

He had to admire the way she did not weep or cry out. She simply turned her back and sat down on the upright chair, a stately little figure, her face hidden by her frivolous bonnet.

Frederica's eyes searched frantically round the room for a weapon. She spoke again to try to gain time. "Who is paying you?" she repeated. "Who hates me so much?"

Still he avoided her questions. "I am going to get some provisions," he said gruffly. "We shall deal comfortably together, you shall see." And with that, he went out, carefully locking the door behind him.

As soon as his footsteps had died away, Frederica began to search for a means of escape. With a sob of relief, she remembered the large lethal hatpin which secured her bonnet to her head. She drew it out and looked at it. It winked evilly in the gloom. At least it would furnish some sort of weapon. She tried to use it to prise open the window but the weathered and warped frame held solid. She then tried swinging the chair at the window, but it only bounced from the leaded panes.

She sat down again and stared up at the ceiling. A tiny winking diamond of light caught her eye. Could it possibly be daylight? She remembered the heavy, sagging thatch at the front of the inn. Perhaps this part was in disrepair. The inn looked as if it had not been inhabited for a long time.

The ceiling was so low that she could easily reach it by standing on the chair. She pried at the soft plaster with the hatpin and choked as she was surrounded by a fine powder of dust. There was a little more light. She worked feverishly with the hatpin and her nails for what seemed an incredible length of time, listening all the while for the sound of returning footsteps.

With a sudden *crrump,* a great piece of rotting plaster gave way, nearly braining her, and she found herself looking up at the blue summer sky through a wide jagged piece of torn thatch.

Now the problem was how to get up there! She could see, over the edge of the hole, a tall space between the crumbling plaster of the ceiling and the thatched roof above. Mercifully, it had never been turned into an attic.

With feverish strength, she dragged the iron bedstead across the floor until it was under the hole. She placed the chair on the bed and tried to climb up on it. Twice she fell to the floor, then she suddenly thought to tear out the straw mattress and balance the chair on the wooden planks underneath.

Bitten by various vermin which had escaped from the mattress, her arms scratched and her bonnet in ruins, she thrust herself up through the hole and caught at one of the upper beams just before a large part of the ceiling gave way beneath her.

Sobbing and sweating, she found a precarious toehold on a piece of lathe and clutched the slippery edges of the thatch with both hands. How she ever got up onto the roof, she never knew, but the sound of horses hooves drove her to such a desperate effort, she almost seemed to fly. She found herself lying on the dirty thatch on her stomach with her feet in the gutter.

Down below, she could hear the sounds of the Comte moving about the tap. He seemed to be in no hurry to rejoin his captive.

She twisted her head and looked downwards. For such a low building, the ground seemed to be a long way away. Then to her horror, she heard another lump of plaster falling from the ceiling to the room below.

She heard his quick footsteps, then silence, then the sound of retreating footsteps and then she heard her name being called from directly below her.

She twisted her head and looked down again. He was standing in the small weedy yard directly below her, his handsome face alight with amusement.

"I didn't think such a little thing as you would have lion's courage," he called. "But you can't escape now."

With a sinking heart, Frederica noticed a

ladder lying against the Jericho at the end of the yard. Still lying on her stomach, she began to pull herself upwards by grabbing handfuls of the rotting thatch.

Gone were the proprieties of the London salon. Her Grace, the Duchess of Westerland hitched up her skirt and swung one leg over the ridgepole and looked down.

Still laughing, he was climbing slowly towards her. "What a spitfire!" he mocked. "You make the game all the more exciting, my dear."

Frederica looked down the other side. Even if she could escape to the ground, there was nowhere to hide before he caught up with her. Little wisps of smoke rose from the houses of Barnet across the fields. Somewhere a thrush was pouring out his song to the untroubled sky. She turned back abruptly just as the Comte was reaching out a well-shaped white hand to catch her ankle.

She looked down in horror at that hand. It seemed like some crawling and disembodied creature. She seized her hatpin and stabbed down as hard as she could.

He gave a startled yelp of pain and lost his hold on the roof. His boots scrabbled along the slippery thatch trying to find a foothold. His face, white, drawn and startled stared up at her for a second and then disappeared from view. There was a tremendous crash and then absolute silence apart from the sound of Frederica's ragged breathing.

She waited and waited and listened as hard as she could but no sound came from the yard below. She eased herself back down the roof and then slowly down the ladder which the Comte had propped against the side of the house, expecting every minute to hear his hated voice explaining that it had all been a trap.

No one could have possibly been killed by falling such a short distance.

But the Comte had caught his heel in the gutter and had been thrown backwards. His head had struck a woodpile in the yard and he had been knocked unconscious. He lay motionless with his eyes closed and his mouth open.

Frederica edged past him with trembling legs, frightened that he would suddenly rise up to mock her. She heard a whinnying and stamping from the side of the house. She stood, irresolute, wondering if she had enough courage left to take one of the horses. But all the strength seemed to have left her arms, and she did not know the first thing about harnessing a horse.

The Comte gave a faint groan and she took to her heels, racing through the tap, out of the inn door, across the road and into the fields.

She did not slow her pace until she had left the inn far behind.

She had a long time to think as she trudged wearily across the fields in the direction of Barnet. Much as she wanted to reject it, an idea was taking shape in her mind. Surely the only person who might wish her disgraced was her husband. Divorce was rare but not impossible. Perhaps he still longed to marry Clarissa and what better way to get out of a distasteful marriage but to prove his wife a slut. And what did she know of this man? They had hardly been alone together, even for breakfast, since the day they were wed. And at Chartsay, he had always seemed to be in the company of Clarissa.

Tears began to run down her dusty cheeks. But where could she run to? As she plodded on, a slow burning anger began to drive away her grief.

She would hire a chaise in Barnet and return to London. She was to attend a ball at Almack's Assembly rooms in King Street that very evening. Well, she would be there. If any questions were asked, she would say she had become tired of the Comte's company and had asked him to set her down in

Bond Street so that she might do some shopping. Since Frederica, with all the privileges of a young married woman, often dispersed with her maid on shopping expeditions, no one would think it odd. No matter what pain and effort it took, she would never mention the episode to anyone.

In her rage over her husband's supposed guilt, she hardly spared a thought for the injured Comte.

The Duke and Chuffy had made exhaustive enquiries throughout Barnet while Frederica was still abroad in the fields. Lots of carriages had gone through, said people shaking their heads. This was one of the busiest roads in England. And who could say which lady had been milord's wife?

Tired and dusty the pair halted at a posting house to rest their weary horses. Pegasus was munching oranges with his eyes closed in ecstacy. "Would *die* for 'em," said Chuffy Pellington-James proudly to explain his ancient animal's stamina. The Duke was looking strained and worried.

"You know what I think," said Chuffy cautiously.

"No. What?"

"I think the Duchess never went to Barnet. That's what I think. Lay you a

171

monkey, she's sittin' now in Grosvenor Square."

The Duke's stern look lightened. "I think you may be right," he said slowly.

"And," pursued Chuffy, "he probably made up that fake letter from the Jennington's so's to get an opportunity to drive out with her. Probably didn't have anything more sinister in mind."

"Why on earth would he do that?"

Chuffy looked at him peculiarly. "Well, me bucko, your wife is a deuced pretty little thing. All the crack. Told you so. Everyone's copying her style. Lots of females have stopped cuttin' and frizzin' their hair 'cause of her."

The Duke looked at him in surprise. "Little Frederica? I would never have believed it. But . . . yes . . . now you mention it, she does look remarkably well on occasion."

Chuffy looked solemnly at his horse as if for inspiration. What a curst rum marriage!

When the weary pair returned to Grosvenor Square late that evening, after giving their horses a long rest before embarking on the road home, it was to find that the Duchess had indeed left for Almack's.

They did not know that while they rested at the one posting house, a ragged and battered Frederica was hiring a chaise at a rival establishment, fortunately having enough money in her purse to pay for it in advance.

Frederica had learned of her husband's return and was more than ever determined to keep up appearances. Long gloves hid the scratches and bruises on her arm and rouge disguised the pallor of her cheeks.

It seemed to the Duke that Frederica had learned of his return and had not even troubled to wait for him. By the time he was dressed in his evening clothes, he was in a towering rage.

What the famous assembly rooms of Almack lacked in appearance, being a set of singularly unpretentious rooms, was more than made up for by the sparkling glamour of the guests' gowns and jewels. The news of the Duke's return to town had already been whispered about and curious eyes followed the little Duchess as she danced with admirer after admirer with a hectic glint in her eyes.

Jack Ferrand was first to see her and, being the most unobtrusive of gentlemen, none noticed his hurried flight from the ballroom.

Frederica might have heard of her husband's frantic search for her had Chuffy Pellington-James been able to arrive in time. But that social gentleman had dropped in at his club on the road to chat with his cronies and to display the glory of his new swansdown waistcoat. Even the elegant Mr. Brummell had only declared it to be "startling but unseasonable," instead of delivering himself of one of his more famous setdowns.

Chuffy was enjoying a cheroot and watching the play at one of the tables when one of his rivals in the Dandy set, young Lord Sackett, minced up to him.

"Pon rep, if you ain't the downy one," he lisped and then sniggered and patted Chuffy on the waistcoat. "Downy! Get it."

"Don't want it," said Chuffy huffily, trying to move away.

But his tormentor pursued him along the table. "You won't be able to squire the pretty Duchess around anywhere now that the Duke is back," he said.

"The Duke is as dear to me as the Duchess," said Chuffy acidly, striking the palm of his chubby hand against his heart to emphasise the point.

"Dear me, how touching," sniggered Lord Sackett. Like a hound he sniffed the air with his small pointed nose. "Dear me! *What* a ghastly smell. You should tell your man not to overheat the curling tongs so much."

"I don't need curling tongs," complained Chuffy, speaking the absolute truth, since he was wearing his blonde wig.

"Then what the dooce is that demned odor," pouted his rival. "Let me see . . . reminds me of Christmas in the kithens. Cleaning the goose? No. Plucking the goose? No. Aha, I've got it. Singeing the feathers. Why, you silly chump."

Chuffy looked slowly downwards after sending a fervent prayer up to whatever fickle God looked after the Tulips of the *ton* and the pain in his hand almost matched the pain of wounded vanity in his large breast. He had crushed his cheroot into his precious waistcoat over his heart and now a dark brown smoking hole was spreading over the snowy-white down.

His agonies were not over. Before he could beat a retreat, the elderly Earl of Durr who was playing piquet at the table in front of Chuffy turned round abruptly and barked, "Damme, man! Don't you know you're on fire?" And seizing his glass of Madeira, the noble Earl threw the contents straight onto Chuffy's massive bosom.

Gathering the rags of his dignity and his waistcoat about his large form, Chuffy teetered off to change again for the ball.

Too late to secure Frederica for a dance, he contented himself by rocking back and forth on his preposterously high heels at the edge of the ballroom floor and mourning his lost waistcoat.

His lugubrious face brightened at the arrival of the Duke of Westerland. It was not often that members of the Corinthian set favored him with their friendship, and he had sensed in the tall Duke a kindness of spirit not often to be found in the members of his own set.

He titupped forward eagerly, missed his footing on the polished floor, and prostrated himself at the feet of one of the patronesses, Sally, Lady Jersey.

"There is no need to go to such extremes, Mr. Pellington-James," trilled Lady Jersey. "A simple bow would be quite enough, I can assure you." Then she ran away, flitting from group to group, her high voice carrying back to Chuffy's red ears, "And, *my dear*. Isn't it *killing*. I said, 'A simple bow will be enough . . .' "

Poor Chuffy. He longed to pour his troubles into some sympathetic ear and looked for Frederica, but she was now dancing with her husband. Both were waltzing beautifully, both were looking at each other with hard, glittering smiles and both were obviously furious. It says a lot for Chuffy's large and generous heart that this sight distressed him more than any of the humiliations of the evening.

"Well, madame," the Duke was saying. "And did you not consider it important to wait at home for my arrival?"

"You did not ever care to write and tell me of your arrival," snapped Frederica. "You expect too much, sir."

"And what about this Comte you have been parading round with?" he demanded, doubly angry now that she had made him feel guilty.

"Oh, the Comte," said Frederica faintly. She had a sudden vision of the Comte lying unconscious in the inn yard and the awful reality that she had a dangerous enemy — probably her husband — who would strike again.

She turned deathly white and swayed on her feet. "I have the headache," she gasped. "Please take me home."

The Duke bit back the angry remarks on his lips. What was there about this Comte which should make her so upset? But she looked indeed ill and he led her silently from the ballroom.

Silently they swayed side by side in their carriage through the dark London streets.

Silently they separated and went off to their respective rooms.

They could not have been further apart had Jack Ferrand's plot to compromise her with the Comte succeeded.

Chapter Nine

The long summer passed, the Little Season began, and four people were absent from the social scene.

The Duke of Westerland, it was rumored, had thrown himself into modern agriculture in a way unheard of since the days of "Turnip" Townshend.

The Honorable Jack Ferrand had ridden to Barnet on the night of the ball at Almack's to find the Comte nursing a bandaged head in the parlor of the posting house where Frederica had hired her chaise. He had ordered him to return immediately to France which the Comte promised to do . . . only after he had forced Mr. Ferrand to pay him a considerable sum to keep his mouth shut.

There was nothing left for Jack Ferrand to do but retire to his estates, increase the tenant's taxes — to compensate for the sum paid to the Comte — and plan his next move.

Clarissa kept him informed by post of the cheering coldness in the ducal marriage.

And Frederica, Duchess of Westerland, had discovered the joys of reading.

Her youthful education had been scant. She had been allowed to benefit from the crumbs of wisdom left over from Clarissa's tutoring — the fundamentals of reading and writing, some little use of the globes, needlework, water-color painting, and a little tutoring on the pianoforte. Once she discovered the little-used library at the back of the Grosvenor Square house she had plunged into an orgy of reading.

Now instead of boxes from the dressmaker, boxes of books appeared from Hatchard's in Piccadilly. The other world held between the book covers removed her temporarily from the bitter reality of her own.

But time had passed and the nightmare of the Comte's perfidy had begun to recede. The little she saw of her husband was at least enough to convince her that he certainly did not seem to hate her. In fact, he hardly seemed to notice her at all.

She began to wish she had confided in him. But she had since learned that ladies of the ton did not casually accept invitations to drive out unescorted unless they were setting up a new flirt. The more she reviewed her behavior, the crazier it seemed . . . and the crazier the Comte seemed. Perhaps there had been no plot against her at all and the Comte had simply been deranged. In a tranquil world composed of eating, sleeping, and reading, Frederica barely saw a soul, although sometimes Mr. Pellington-James dropped by to take tea, patently sad that the dashing Duchess showed no signs of dash any more.

He had decided to court Clarissa who was once again the reigning belle of the London scene, but she had laughed at him so cruelly that he quickly retired from the lists.

One wintry afternoon, when Frederica was happily esconced in front of a blazing fire in the library, Mr. Pellington-James positively burst into the room, triumphantly waving two tickets.

"Now you have got to come out of seclusion," he cried. "I have purchased — at great expense, mind you — two tickets to see Romeo Coates."

"Who on earth is Romeo Coates?" asked Frederica, putting down her book with a reluctant sigh. "A prize fighter?"

Chuffy raised his eyebrows and his hands in horror. "You have been out of the world too long. Romeo Coates. Diamond Coates. Curricle Coates. The Gifted Amateur."

"What a lot of titles the gentleman seems

to have amassed," interrupted Frederica. "Who is he?"

"He is the newest rage," cried Chuffy. "He is playing Romeo at the Haymarket tonight." He went on to explain that Romeo Coates was in fact a Mr. Robert Coates of the West Indies who had achieved such fame in the part of Romeo that he had become known as Romeo Coates. He was one of the most famous sights of Long Acre as he flashed past in his scallop-shaped chariot, bedecked in furs and diamonds. Chuffy had gone through extraordinary machinations to procure the tickets. She just had to come.

Frederica hesitated. She had never seen Shakespeare performed on the stage although she had read almost all his plays during the last few months. But with a new-found awareness of the necessary proprieties attached to the title of Duchess, she said tentatively, "I do not know whether I should accept. My husband is at home and . . ."

"Oh, that's all right," said Chuffy. "Met Henry on the way in and told him about it. He lets me call him Henry, you know. And he said he had no objections to me squiring you."

"Really? I have indeed a sweet and understanding husband," said Frederica acidly.

But Chuffy was impervious to sarcasm. "Good! That's settled. I have bought a whole new outfit for the occasion. You won't be able to believe your eyes."

He was right — Frederica could *not* believe her eyes when Chuffy proudly presented himself in the drawing room that evening.

He was dressed from head to foot in white silk. He wore a white silk jacket, white silk waistcoat and white silk knee breeches. Diamond brooches and buckles were pinned indiscriminately over his large form, and he wore a heavy powdered wig. He looked like a heavenly footman.

Frederica, who had been untroubled by eccentricity when she had been cutting a dash in town now felt unaccountably shy. She had not wanted to be so noticeable on her first evening back in society. But Chuffy looked so radiantly pleased with his appearance, she had not the heart to disappoint him. With an innate sense of style she realized that if she dressed as extravagantly as Chuffy, he would somehow appear less ridiculous.

Chuffy had arrived early so she urged him to wait while she changed.

The Westerland family diamonds, reset

and cleaned, had been presented to her by the Duke — that is, thought Frederica wryly, if one could consider handing them to the butler with a curt note, presenting them.

She chose an as-yet unworn ballgown of white silk with a silver gauze overdress and allowed her maid to clasp the heavy diamond collar round her neck. Her hairdresser redressed her hair in a suitable style to set off the little fairy-tale diamond tiara.

Chuffy's eyes misted over with tears when he saw her. "Oh, wait till Lord Sackett sees us," he gasped. "We shall be the cynosure, my dear Duchess."

But startling as their appearance was, London Society was not far behind. The little theater was ablaze with jewels sparkling on men and women alike. It was packed to capacity and Frederica noticed with surprise that the rowdier of the Corinthian set had turned out in full force. She was puzzled. They would surely have been more at home in the cock-pit than at the performance of a Shakespeare play. Yet after Mr. Coates' first entrance which was greeted with tumultuous cheers and cat calls, she began to understand why.

He was a most ridiculous, if magnificently dressed, figure.

He wore a species of silk, woven so as to give it the appearance of silver, and he was plastered with diamonds. He appeared inordinately fond of his legs which were encased in pink silk stockings. He kept holding up the action of the play by walking to the front of the stage to present his legs to their best advantage.

Such of the lines as she was able to hear above the noise were new to Frederica. "I do not recognize it," she whispered to Chuffy. "Is it not Shakespeare then?"

Chuffy whispered back that Mr. Coates had said that he knew the Shakespeare play by heart but had been reported to have remarked airily, "I think I have improved on it."

He had a most peculiar accent. Perfect was pronounced "purfet", burden "barden", and memory "memmary".

He was mercilessly heckled by the boxes and would select the noisiest of his tormentors by pointing straight at their box and delivering himself of David Garrick's famous lines:

"Ye bucks of the boxes who roar and reel,
Too drunk to listen and too proud to feel."

Frederica was beginning to wish she had not come. The noise became deafening as a

185

chorus of cockcrows arose from the pit. The unfortunate actor had chosen as his crest a cock with outspread wings and the motto, "While I live, I'll crow."

At the interval, Frederica saw Emily and her fiance, Archie Hefford, in one of the boxes opposite. She would have gone to visit them but Mr. Pellington-James advised her to stay. It was getting very rowdy, he told Frederica, and he wished he had not brought her. He, for one, could not understand the rude behaviour of the audience. Romeo Coates was the finest actor he had ever seen. Why . . . there was the Duke!

A moment later, poor Chuffy could have bitten off his tongue. He began to say that he had been mistaken but Frederica had already spied her husband in one of the lower boxes along with the fair charmer at his side. The girl was as young as Frederica but as blonde and beautiful as Clarissa.

The curtain mercifully arose again and she turned a rigid face to the stage. Her nightmare had just begun. Mr. Coates, it seemed, approved of the diamond-covered spectacle presented by Chuffy and Frederica, and played all his lines to their box. As Chuffy had promised, they were indeed the cynosure, but not in the way he expected.

The play survived into the fifth act when the sight of Romeo trying to break into Juliet's tomb with a crowbar proved too much for the audience. Some women laughed so much they became hysterical and had to be carried out.

At long last, Romeo decided to die. He carefully dusted the stage with his handkerchief, spread the handkerchief out carefully, placed his expensive hat on it, and deigned finally to lie down on the stage.

This was greeted with a great ironic burst of applause whereupon Romeo solemnly rose to life, advanced towards the orchestra with a smug smile, and carefully arranged his legs in what he considered was their best position. Then he returned to die again, this time over the body of the unfortunate Juliet who was crying gustily with humiliation despite the fact that she was being paid double to endure the ordeal.

The curtain at last swung down and the house lights were lit. Of the Duke and his fair partner, there was no sign.

The couple made their way back to Grosvenor Square in silence. Chuffy felt terribly guilty. Lord Sackett had told him that Romeo Coates was the best actor in the world and now he felt he had been made a fool of, though, for his part, he could see nothing wrong with the fellow.

He stole a cautious look at his young companion. What on earth had made the Duke turn up at the play with that lightskirt? And he knew that Frederica was to be there — Chuffy himself had told him.

Frederica was terribly angry. When she considered the incredible effort it had taken her to go about as if nothing had happened after the Comte's abduction in order to protect the name of Westerland, and when she considered the long restless nights of nightmares where the Comte's green eyes had come to haunt her, and all to be suffered alone, she felt like strangling the handsome Duke.

Giving poor Chuffy an abrupt goodnight, she swept into the mansion only to find that her husband had not yet returned. "When His Grace returns," she told the startled butler, "please inform him that I am in the library."

Still dressed in her finery, she ordered the fire in the library to be made up and prepared to wait.

It was three o'clock in the morning before the Duke fumbled his way into the hallway of his home. Worthing, the butler, informed him in hushed tones that Her Grace was waiting for him in the library and watched with anxious eyes as His Grace tacked across the hall in that direction.

The Duke had never been so drunk in his life, or so angry. He had planned to revenge himself on Frederica for her cold silences and snubs by appearing at the play with that particular bit of muslin on his arm. But somehow it had all rebounded when he caught a glimpse of her horrified face across the theater. She should not expect him to behave like a monk. The small voice of conscience telling him that she had every right to expect him to keep his amours from the public eye made him even angrier.

He pushed open the library door and went in. His wife was lying asleep in a chair by the fire. Her small face under the blazing and flashing tiara looked very young and vulnerable.

He stirred up the fire and threw on a shovelful of coal. The noise awoke her and she looked up into her husband's face. He looked very handsome and debonair and she smiled at him sleepily.

Then her eyes focussed on a stain of rouge on his cravat and her face hardened and she sat bolt upright.

"Will you kindly explain your behavior this evening, sir?" she demanded imperiously. "And am I to expect such behavior in the future? Are you going to flaunt your lightskirts in front of me?"

"Yes," he said casually, tapping his fingers lightly on the bookshelves. "So long as you are content to behave like a nun, do not expect me to behave like a monk."

Frederica was shaking with anger. "It is as well I found out about your amours in time, my lord Duke. Only think what might have happened to me had I decided to share your bed."

"What are you talking about? What could happen to you?"

"The pox," said Frederica, clearly and distinctly.

Shock sobered him momentarily. "I will have you know, madame, that the ladies I consort with are diamonds of the first water and, above all, clean. You have furthermore no right to know about such things."

"Hah!" sneered his wife. "It is just as well I do."

"I have no doubt that you have been well taught by your gallants," he said. "It is as well you do not share my bed, madame, I have no taste for Haymarket ware."

"Nonsense!" replied his little wife, looking him up and down. "That is the only type of female you know how to deal with . . . that is with the exception of dear Clarissa whom, of course, you positively worship."

"Clarissa is a common little slut and so are you," remarked her husband in a conversational voice.

The hard and bitter words were building up enormous barriers between them but both were too proud to try to conciliate the other.

The Duke weaved slightly and clutched at the mantle for support.

"You're bosky," said Frederica bitterly. What had happened to the gallant and charming Captain Wright? He stood glaring down at her, the red lights from the fire glinting in his eyes.

"On the other hand," he said, "I may as well have a sample of what you have been giving away so freely."

He pulled her to him and kissed her hard on the mouth. He smelled of wine and cheap perfume.

Frederica tore herself free and wiped the back of her hand across her mouth. "I am leaving you, sir. You are too drunk to know what you are doing."

She turned towards the door and he lunged after her. She twisted, eluding his grasp, and then ran as hard as she could up the stairs. Avoiding her rooms, she ran to the top of the house and hid in one of the attics. She heard him roaring her name, she heard doors being thrown open, and then there was blessed silence.

She found she was trembling with shock. She rose on shaky legs and made her way down to her bedroom. From the gossip at the tea tables, she had gathered that a drunken husband was a common occurrence in this hard-drinking society. Women of her acquaintance seemed to cope with an elegant shrug. Men, it seemed, were not men unless they crawled home in the small hours on their hands and knees. Why, even the Prince Regent was reported to have spent his wedding night with his head in the fire-irons — although the gossips said that his mistress, Mrs. Fitzherbert, had put a sedative in his wine.

But Frederica had considered her husband to be far above such behavior. She was bitterly disappointed in him and considered herself well out of the agonies of love. Tomorrow, her coldness would not be affected. It would be a part of her soul.

With a cold courage, she started the next day, confident that she would be spared her husband's presence at the breakfast table. But to her horror, he was already there and obviously waiting for her before he went out. Beau Brummell, that arbiter of fashion, had damned the masculine wear of knee breeches and swallow-tail coats for day wear since they were affected by Bonaparte and his rabble of commoners. The Duke was all the crack in a silk frogged coat lined with beaver and biscuit colored pantaloons. He was wearing his snowy cravat in the style known as Trone d'Amour — well starched and with one single horizontal dent in the middle.

He had already breakfasted and was obviously prepared to go out.

He knew that his little wife did not speak French so it was impossible to carry on conversation in front of the servants. He waited until her plate was filled and then with a wave of his hand dismissed them.

His wife's long heavy hair had been piled on top of her head in a style that was entirely her own. Her slim, girlish figure was able to carry the current mode of gown — which was padded in the front to make the wearer look about six months pregnant — without appearing ridiculous.

Frederica choked some toast down her dry throat and desperately wished he would go away.

She reached forward for another piece of toast and his long thin fingers closed over her wrist. "Please look at me, Frederica," he said in a soft voice.

"I am truly sorry for my behavior last night. I got in with a pretty hard-drinking set at Watier's yesterday and won quite a sum of money and the tickets to the Haymarket Theater. Sackett was drunker than I and he began to bait me about my wife's gallants. He was hoping to hurt me and to start a quarrel with Chuffy. I told him that I was fully aware that Mr. Pellington-James was a friend of my wife's and that I was grateful to him for squiring her when I was gone from town. He began to imply that I was a cuckold and I challenged him to a duel. Don't worry," he added as Frederica gave a gasp of horror. "He did not accept the challenge. I am accounted a pretty fair shot.

"I decided to walk from Watier's to the Haymarket and the fresh air, combined with the wine I had drunk, addled my wits and I began to become furious with you, my dear. I felt that it was all your fault that I had been put in this humiliating position. I wanted to humiliate you in return. I called on a certain ladybird I used to know and begged her to accompany me. I only succeeded in humiliating myself further. I took her home and then repaired to Brook's where I made myself further obnoxious by insulting all the Whigs. The Beau took me aside and told me there was absolutely no *veritas* in *vino* and told me to go home. I challenged *him* to a duel to which he replied, 'Good God, certainly not!' My humiliation was complete.

"I am extremely sorry, my dear. Please forgive me."

Black eyes met grey ones for a long moment while poor Frederica fell more in love with her husband than ever.

"Of course I forgive you," she remarked truthfully. "But I would still like to know, sir, how you came to be reeking of cheap perfume and how you got that rouge on your cravat?"

He had the grace to blush. "My . . . er . . . lady friend tried to detain me when I took her home."

"You are a terrible man," said Frederica lightly.

"It was all caused by Sackett's jealousy of Chuffy. That Dandy set spit and fight like cats over who has the best waistcoat. By the way, did you hear what happened to poor Chuffy?"

She shook her head and so he told her the fate of the swansdown waistcoat and made her laugh.

"There!" he cried. "That is more like my Frederica."

He smiled into her eyes, those large black eyes with the little gold flecks, which held his own with such an expression of . . . of what? "What are your plans for the day?"

Frederica hesitated a little. "I had planned to drive with Mr. Pellington-James but if you would rather not . . ."

"No, no," he laughed. "Chuffy is the best of men. You must forgive my jealousy of last night . . ."

Frederica looked at him with a gleam of hope. Jealousy?

"You know what men are like," he teased, "when it comes to their wives. Like dogs with bones."

"Oh!" said Frederica in a small voice.

"We shall be going to the Queen's House together this evening?" When she nodded her assent, he suddenly bent and kissed her lightly on the cheek and then left.

When Chuffy arrived she was still holding her hand to her cheek and staring in a bemused way at the door.

Frederica hurriedly made her apologies and ran to change. When she returned, she was dressed in a blue velvet carriage dress with a fur lined blue velvet coat and an enormous swansdown muff.

The only thing warm about Chuffy's dress was his cravat which was tied in the Mail Coach, a style, according to the publisher Stockdale, in his pamphlet "Neckclothitania, or Tietania: Being an Essay on Starches," worn by "all stage-coachmen, guards, the *swells* of the *fancy* and Ruffians." It consisted of a large Cashmere shawl with one end brought over the knot, spread out and tucked into the waist. It was mostly worn with the many-capered livery of the Four-in-Hand Club but Chuffy had elected to sport it with a jacket of the thinnest silk, skin-tight leather breeches and boots with white tops.

London was grey and black and bitter cold. Chuffy decided that they should take a short drive round St. James's Park and then return. He accordingly edged his chariot in that direction through the press of traffic. London seemed to be bursting at the seams and the hotels were crowded. Stephen's in Bond Street was full of the army, Ibbetson's crammed with undergraduates and clergy, the Clarendon with gourmets, and fusty and dreary Limmer's chock-ablock with country squires and race course touts. At last they reached St. James's Park and Chuffy reined in so that Frederica could admire the view.

Still thinking of her husband Frederica looked around vaguely at the desolate park. Fog was beginning to creep towards them as if pale ghosts were emanating from the

Queen's House at the other end. It hardly merited the title of 'park,' being a long dirty field intersected by a wide dirty ditch and thinly planted with rotting lime trees.

Chuffy shivered in his thin silk and once again mourned the loss of his swansdown waistcoat. He had never had the heart to order another. What a terrible day that had been with the long ride to Barnet and then tripping and falling in front of Lady Jersey at Almack's. But good old Pegasus. Even the Duke had been amazed at the old animal's stamina. "Do *anything* for oranges," said Chuffy dreamily.

"Who?" asked Frederica, turning her eyes away from the gloomy view.

"Pegasus. M'horse. Henry couldn't believe the way Pegasus flew up that hill to Barnet when we was lookin' for you."

A cold hand clutched at Frederica's heart.

"When did you go to Barnet?" she asked.

"Didn't I tell you? Suppose not. After the accident to my waistcoat, damme if everything else wasn't driven out of my head. It hurts a chap deep when things like that happen. Did I ever tell you of . . ."

"Yes," said Frederica. "Why were you in Barnet?"

"Lookin' for you," said Chuffy, surprised. "When the Duke came back from Scotland,

198

he says, 'Where is my wife?' I said, 'I don't know. Think she's gone to Richmond with that Comte fellow.' He said, 'What?' I said, 'The Comte Duchesne.' He said, 'Never heard of him.' I said . . .' "

"Oh, get to the *point*," screamed Frederica, scaring a covey of mallards out of the rushes.

Chuffy looked at her in surprise. "I *was* getting to the point but if you're goin' to shout at me. . . ."

"I am not shouting," shouted Frederica and then, forcibly calming herself, she went on in a gentle voice, "Dear Chuffy, just tell me simply why you and my husband went to Barnet."

"Well, to look for you, o'course," remarked Chuffy. "Told Henry I thought the Comte looked a havey-cavey fellow and he had faked that letter from the Jenningtons and we went off to Barnet but couldn't find you."

"How did you know I had gone to Barnet?" asked Frederica quietly.

"I can't remember. I suppose Henry knew somehow," said Chuffy, forgetting all about the visit to Clarissa.

Frederica sat as if turned to stone. If her husband had known she had gone to Barnet then he must have known about the

Comte . . . even have paid the Comte. . . .

"But you should have seen old Pegasus," Chuffy went on. "Do anything for oranges that old boy would. Hey! It's getting demned foggy. Let us go back."

But he felt a small gloved hand on his arm and, turning, he saw his young companion's face was wet with tears.

"Oh, I say," bleated Chuffy. "What did I say? Don't you *like* horses?"

Frederica smiled wanly through her tears. "I want to stay and think for a bit, Chuffy. Please."

Chuffy shivered but was too much of a gentleman to protest. Great yellow clouds were blotting everything from sight and a fine rain of soot was beginning to fall on his wrist bands. His hands under their York tan gloves seemed to be frozen to the reins.

He suddenly spied wavering lights approaching them in the fog and cursed under his breath. In no time at all, a gang of ruffians was upon them, the horses seized by the reins and the carriage encircled by the most evil group of vagabonds Frederica had ever seen, their faces flickering like demons in the light of the flaring tar torches they carried.

"Here's a fine pair o' gentry morts for the plucking!" cried the leader. His red eyes gleamed in his pockmarked face and his clothes, like those of his band, were no better than a series of rags held together by a rope round the waist. They were armed with cudgels and chains and their faces were alight with savage glee.

"Let's get rid o' the fat 'un and then we'll have our fun with the moll," said the leader placing his greasy, grimy hand appreciatively on the fine silk of Chuffy's sleeve.

Chuffy shook him off and held up his chubby hand. "Now, look here, gentlemen. Have you ever seen a man of quality undress?" And without waiting for a reply, he started to calmly divest himself of his boots which he threw to the crowd. Frederica thought Chuffy had gone mad . . . as did their tormenters. "Three cheers for the fat 'un," roared the leader. "This is better 'n Bartholomew Fair!"

Surrounded by the grinning faces, Chuffy solemnly removed his silk jacket next and threw it down while the ruffians scrabbled and fought over it like dogs. Then he held up his diamond stick pin so that it winked in the light of the flaring, smoking torches. They watched it as if hypnotised and then Chuffy swung it high above his head and threw it as far as he could. He had meant them all to run after it but the leader stayed

201

beside them and the two men holding the horses stayed firm. Quick as lightning, moving with an incredible speed for so fat a man, Chuffy drew his dress sword and leapt down on the leader and ran him through.

He screamed in his death agony and the others came running back as he fought to pull his sword free. Frederica saw the leader's torch lying on the ground and jumped down from the carriage and seized it, swinging it in a great blazing arc as the ring of faces closed in on them. Chuffy managed to wound two more before he was brought down by a massive blow from a cudgel.

Frederica was left alone. She bravely swung the torch at the circle of men as they closed around her as if keeping a pack of savage wolves at bay. One finally nipped under the fiery arc and, hooking his hand round her neck, pulled her to the ground. Frederica closed her eyes and prayed for a quick death. The stink of bodies as they pressed over her was nigh unbearable.

In final desperation, she found her voice and screamed and screamed. There was a sound of thudding hooves. Leaping down from his horse with his sword in his hand came the Duke with two of his grooms similarly armed. His sword flashed like quicksilver as he brought down two of the ruffians and routed the rest who disappeared off into the yellow curtain of fog like so many demons fleeing back to hell before an avenging angel.

He lifted Frederica very gently to her feet and held her to him for a long moment. "What in hell's name," he said in a thin voice, "were you and Chuffy doing ambling around St. James's in this fog? If one of my grooms hadn't spied you earlier, I wouldn't have known where to look."

"I was sitting thinking," started Frederica when a low groan made them both turn around.

Chuffy crawled to his feet and with a polite, "Please excuse me," tottered round the far side of the carriage where he was heard being desperately ill.

"Help him into the carriage," snapped the Duke. "We will have this out at home."

The Duke took the reins and drove the sorry pair back to Grosvenor Square. His self control was such that he did not begin his interrogation until Chuffy's wounds had been bathed and dressed and Frederica had washed and changed.

"Now," he said sternly, putting a bumper of brandy into Chuffy's hand. "An explanation if you please."

"The Duchess said she wanted to think about something," said Chuffy, "and she was crying. Hope it wasn't anything I said. I was only talking about horses and I know that can bore some ladies to tears. Well, figuratively speakin', that is, never *seen* any of 'em actually cry before but still . . ."

"Will you get to the point," said the Duke testily.

"You know something," said Chuffy with an air of great enlightenment, "you're very like your wife, damme if you ain't. Well, as I was sayin', we just sat there in the fog until that band of ruffians turned up. By God, you were splendid, Duchess. The way you fought those men and held them off with that torch."

"Oh, Chuffy," cried Frederica, "it was you who were marvelous. The way you sprang from the carriage to kill that horrible man."

"If I may interrupt this mutual admiration society," said the Duke coldly, "I would like to point out that you both behaved as if you had windmills in your heads. Do you realize, Chuffy, that if any other man were involved in this and I had been told you had been sitting alone in the middle of a fog dreaming, I would have assumed that you were so far gone in love that you didn't even notice."

"But you wouldn't think that about me?" asked Chuffy plaintively.

The Duke laughed with sudden relief. "Chuffy, my boy, one of these days someone is going to think that about you. You seemed to have behaved very creditably. I didn't know you were a man of action."

"Well, I was for a bit," said Chuffy. "Although at one time I thought I'd never see any. I was in the China Tenth."

"What an odd name for a regiment," interrupted Frederica.

"Well, we was called that because of the Prince being our Colonel — we was supposed to be handled like porcelain, you know. But of course when he became Regent and couldn't fight with us that was when the fun began. We were renamed the Hussars and sent to the Peninsula."

"Were you, By George!" cried the Duke.

His face was alight with boyish enthusiasm as he refilled Chuffy's glass. Both men plunged into reminiscences of their army days and Frederica realized that this was one of those occasions on which even the most attractive women go unnoticed. When she left them, they were sitting in front of the fire using chess pieces and snuff boxes as armies and battalions, obviously the greatest of friends.

A little of her fear had left her as she retired to her rooms. Had her husband wanted rid of her, he would never have ridden to her rescue. She remembered the feel of his arms about her and hugged that thought to her like a talisman for the rest of the day.

Chapter Ten

The great fog still rolled around London in huge billowing, choking clouds. Footmen were dispatched to St. James's to see if the Queen still meant to hold her reception. The Queen most certainly did and social London braced itself for the ordeal.

The Duke and Duchess, arrayed in court dress, sat patiently in their carriage in the long queue of carriages which stretched from the Queen's House all the way down through the park. It was a different scene from the one Frederica had looked at earlier in the day. The flaring torches of the out-riders blazed dimly in the fog as the cream of the top ten thousand waited as patiently as the beggars in the East End waited in the bread line.

Frederica was wearing the regulation court dress of black muslin over an underslip of rose sarcanet and the Duke was attired in black knee breeches and coat and carried his tricorne under his arm. From time to time he eased his neck in its high starched cravat and cursed the delay.

"What do you call that one?" she enquired.

"This, my dear," said the Duke, trying to twist his head to look at her, "is a hellish invention which is a cross between the Irish and the Mathematical — two collateral dents and two horizontal ones. Life was easier before Beau Brummell discovered the starched cravat."

"What an incredible amount of social power Mr. Brummell has, to be sure," remarked Frederica as the carriage slowly inched its way forward. "Really, it looks as if we shall never get there. Is the Little Season usually so busy?"

"Not usually," yawned the Duke. "That's Brummell again. He keeps in town as much as possible, having a dread of cold country houses and blood sports . . . although he can be a damned arrogant puppy when he *is* in the country.

"Archie Hefford was staying at a country home once when Brummell was a guest. Well, the servant was conducting Brummell to the chilly upper rooms where the bachelors are usually put when Brummell halted and said, 'Stop! I cannot go up and down these infernal stairs! Is there no room lower? Here for example?' He opened a door into a very comfortable bedroom. The servant explained that this part of the house was reserved for married couples and this room for an earl. 'The single gentlemen's apartments are . . .' 'I know! I know!' said Brummell. 'So put the earl in one of them — he is a bachelor. There — bring my portmanteau and dressing case.'

"Well, he was getting ready for dinner when there was a knock on the door and the earl called angrily, 'Mr. Brummell! Mr. Brummell!' 'My Lord!' Brummell shouted back, 'I am dressing and cannot be disturbed. I am in my buffs, *in naturabulis*.' 'But this is my room, sir!' yelled the earl. 'Possession, My Lord! Possession!' Brummell replied. 'You know the rest! You are single, My Lord. I am a married man. Married to the gout.' The earl went meekly off and found a room elsewhere."

Frederica laughed. "Mr. Brummell seems such a quiet gentleman."

"Oh, he can be quite a rake-hell when he chooses," smiled the Duke, "especially now he's out of favor with Prinny. Where on earth are we now?" He peered through the carriage window. "The entrance lodge, thank God!"

But it took them a further two and a half hours to get through the colonnade and to the foot of the grand staircase. The heat and stink were oppressive. Society fought and scrabbled on the stairs to get up and those who had paid their respects fought and scrabbled to get down. Dresses were torn, hats were lost among the multitude of hats lying in piles on the entrance tables, and tempers were frayed. Frederica kept close to her large husband's side, glad of his protection.

At last they reached the top of the stairs and a final thrust from the crowd behind propelled them into the Royal presence where Queen Charlotte sat, forever dipping her finger and thumb into her gold snuff box and mournfully scattering the powder over her small monkey face.

Frederica was too terrified and overawed by the royal lady to hear what the Queen said or what her husband replied. Then back out they went to fight their way down the stairs.

Frederica clung tightly to her husband's arm amid the pushing, jostling, backbiting throng. He turned and smiled down at her, "We should never have come," he said. "This is certainly a day for battles in St. James's."

Frederica laughed back and grey eyes met black for a long moment. Clarissa was pushing her way up the stairs when she saw the exchange of looks.

It was certainly time that Jack Ferrand was recalled from the country. She swayed artistically and fell against the Duke as he passed her and clutched at the lapels of his coat. "I am so sorry, Henry," she breathed, "I am feeling faint."

He handed her over to the care of her mother but not before Clarissa had given him one of her lingering special looks.

The Duke looked round for his wife and then noticed her small figure below him in the throng being pushed and pummelled by the crowd.

With an oath he pushed his way to her side and bundled her into a cloak.

"This isn't mine!" cried Frederica.

"It doesn't matter," he said tersely. "You will never find your own in this crush." He pulled her out into the night air, fastidiously brushing Clarissa's powder from his jacket.

"You really must have a word with your stepsister," he said testily. "Her manner is becoming decidedly forward."

"I must . . . I mean I shall," said Frederica, turning a radiant face up to his.

The Duke ruffled her curls affectionately. What an odd little girl she was to be sure. He had just insulted her stepsister and there she stood looking as if it were Christmas morn.

They proceeded back to Grosvenor

Square in a tired but amicable silence. The Duke hesitated on the steps of their home.

"I promised to play a rubber of piquet with some friends at White's. I would stay with you but you look extremely fatigued after your adventures."

Frederica swallowed her disappointment. She had no claims on his time, after all. "You are right," she yawned. "I shall go to bed directly."

"Perhaps we could spend a quiet evening at home tomorrow night," he said, "instead of all this racketing around."

"Oh, I would love that," cried Frederica. He gave her a brotherly kiss on the cheek, told the coachman that he would walk, and strode off into the night.

Frederica stood motionless, watching the tall figure of her husband until he was swallowed up in the fog.

The first person the Duke was to meet after he had crossed the threshold of White's was no other than Jack Ferrand. He had not heard from Clarissa for some time and was anxious to see how the married couple progressed, or rather, did not progress. The Duke greeted him with extra warmth. He had believed Clarissa's story of Jack Ferrand's proposal and assumed that the poor man had been rejected.

"Well, Duke, how do we go on?" cried Mr. Ferrand. "And I trust your good Duchess is as lovely as ever."

"Lovelier," remarked the Duke simply with a certain warmth in his voice that made Mr. Ferrand narrow his eyes slightly.

But he replied, "Splendid. I shall no doubt have the pleasure of seeing her at the Countess of Buckinghamshire's tomorrow night. Do you attend Albinia's house-warming?"

The Duke smiled. "Thank you for reminding me. I must send our regrets. My wife and I have decided to spend a quiet evening at home together."

Jack Ferrand affected a sudden air of drunken jollity. "Come now, this will never do. If you set the fashion, London will be bereft of pretty ladies. Tell you what. Play you the dice. You win, you stay home. I win, you go to Albinia's."

The Duke laughed and tried to pass by into the gaming room but Jack Ferrand seemed to become drunker and jollier, his friendly, open face positively beaming with goodwill. "I am determined on the wager," he said with an infectious grin.

"Oh, very well," said the good-natured Henry who was used to the mad bets of the more ebullient of his friends.

Like magic, an ebony box of dice appeared on Jack Ferrand's palm. "Don . . . don't worry 'bout the gamingroom," he slurred. "We'll play right here."

The Duke threw and found himself looking at a three and a two. Jack Ferrand threw with a deft turn of the wrist and turned up a pair of sixes. "I win," he crowed. "See you tomorrow night."

The Duke clapped him on the back in a friendly way and recommended the efficacy of several pots of black coffee and went off to join his friends. Archie Hefford rose to meet him. "You'll find yourself out in the street an' you persist in gaming in the hallway."

"Oh, it was only Ferrand, as drunk as a lord," laughed the Duke.

Archie raised his thin eyebrows in surprise. "He looked as sober as a judge just before you came in. Still, there's no telling. How's Frederica? How on earth can she tolerate that fop, Chuffy Pellington-James?"

"Oh, Chuffy's all right," said the Duke easily. "He grows on one."

"Well, he looks as if he's growing over there by the window and Brummell don't like it. It ain't as if he's one of the Bow Window Set, you know. Alvanley told him to

214

move and he simply said 'Can't' and went on staring out into the street like a damned cod's head."

There indeed stood Mr. Pellington-James, resplendent in one of Trufitt's best nutty brown wigs reeking with oil, a prodigiously padded and wasp-waisted evening coat, knee breeches, silk stockings, and the inevitable high heels. His eyes lit up with relief when he saw the Duke approaching.

"Are you stuck or something?" asked the Duke sympathetically.

"It's my coat," whispered Chuffy hoarsely. "It's caught in the window. Flunkey closed it on me before I knew what was happening and I felt such a fool, I didn't like to tell anyone."

"Why didn't you just take off your coat and free yourself," said the Duke reasonably.

"I couldn't," moaned Chuffy. "It took two strong footmen to get me into it."

The Duke grinned and released his fat friend who wheezed with relief like a grampus. "I had better go home," said Chuffy, after thanking him profusely. "Will I see you at the Countess of Buckinghamshire's tomorrow?"

"No, I'm staying home. . . ." The Duke suddenly frowned. "Yes, you will, dammit.

Jack Ferrand was a bit bosky and he wagered me I would go. What on earth made me accept such a curst stupid bet I'll never know."

"He's like that . . . Ferrand, I mean," said Chuffy. "Something about his eyes. Gets a fellow to do the stupidest things. You know what? I don't like him. Somethin' about him makes me feel as if I've just turned over a stone."

"It's that blow on your head, Chuffy," teased the Duke. "Ferrand's one of the most open and easygoing fellows I've come across. Off to bed with you. Hey, wait a minute, I'll introduce you to Brummell."

Mr. Pellington-James had received many samples of the Beau's wit but he had never been formally introduced. His great chest swelled with pride, particularly as he saw the small, venomous face of Lord Sackett peering enviously at him from across the fog-filled room. The famous Beau shook hands and remarked in his light, pleasant voice that he had in fact noticed Mr. Pellington-James on many occasions. His dress was most extraordinarily eye catching. Chuffy beamed and swelled so much that the Duke, being well aware that Beau Brummell was about to deliver one of his famous set downs, urged the beaming and gratified Chuffy from the room.

On his return he noticed Lord Hefford sitting idly at the window, staring out into the fog.

"What's the matter, Archie?" he said looking down at his friend. "Emily's all right isn't she? Wedding all set?"

His friend nodded gloomily. "Oh, everything's all right with Emily, when I see her that is. 'Course you won't know since you've been keeping your head down in the manure at Chartsay, but Emily's got landed with some platter-faced female from the country and everywhere we go, she goes.

"Her name's Priscilla Wheatcroft and I suppose she ain't that bad 'cept she's always underfoot, if you know what I mean. She's terribly shy and wispy and *clings* and is terrified of London. I tried to point out to Mrs. Cholmley that she was supposed to be the chaperone, not me and Emily, and she not only went into that stone deaf act of hers but her butler, Stafford . . . biblical cove . . . *he* pretends he's deaf as well. Priscilla's not pretty enough to *take* or I'd have unloaded her on some unsuspecting acquaintance long ago."

"Well, we must just rack our brains for a suitable gallant," said the Duke. He glanced out the window to where a furred and jewelled Chuffy was being heaved into his chariot by two footmen. "Perhaps," he said slowly, "I know just the fellow . . ."

Frederica looked at her spouse with amazement across the length of the breakfast table. "We *have* to go to Albinia's. But why?"

The Duke could not bring himself to tell her about the wager. "I remembered last night that I had promised her particularly that we would attend."

Frederica would have argued but the butler announced that Mrs. Byles-Bondish had arrived and requested to see Her Grace. He had put her in the Egyptian room. Frederica flushed. She knew that Mrs. Byles-Bondish had come to present some bill or other and she did not have enough experience to cope with such a domineering lady. She trailed off miserably and the Duke looked after her with some surprise. There was a great deal about his wife's private life, he realized, that he did not know. He decided to go and investigate.

Silence fell as he entered the Egyptian room. Mrs. Byles-Bondish looked wary and Frederica flushed scarlet with embarrassment. She was clutching a piece of paper. With a few quick strides, he crossed the room and took it from her nerveless fingers.

"What is this?" he said levelling his quizzing glass. "Rundell & Bridges . . . to cleaning of jewelery . . . but your jewelery had just been cleaned, my dear. I shall call on them personally."

Mrs. Byles-Bondish cleared her throat. "That bill is mine, Your Grace. I get Her Grace to check my accounts from time to time. She has a wonderful head for figures."

The Duke swung the quizzing glass round on Mrs. Byles-Bondish. "You're talking fustian, you know," he said pleasantly. "You were trying to get my wife to frank this."

"Frederica! What other bills have you paid for this person?"

"Oh, just clothes and things like that," whispered Frederica with her head bowed.

The Duke crossed to the door and held it open. "Out!" he commanded. Scarlet with rage, Mrs. Byles-Bondish swept to the door.

"Worthing!" called the Duke to the butler. "Please make sure that this woman is never admitted again."

He went back and sat down opposite his wife who still sat with her head bowed.

"Why did you not tell me that you had been troubled by that encroaching female?"

"I felt ashamed," whispered Frederica. "I

felt I should be able to cope with her on my own but somehow I couldn't."

He took her hands and raised her to her feet. "If anything like that happens again, you must leave it to me," he said gently, putting a stray curl behind her ear.

"There now, don't look so worried. I shan't scold." He bent and kissed her gently on the lips. "It's a nuisance we have go to out tonight. The Countess lives in the King's Road which is a damned inconvenient distance from town without being exactly in the country."

Frederica's heart beat very quickly but she said lightly, "At least it will be a fashionable gathering. I trust none of your West End comets will be present."

"Outrageous minx," he teased. "My West End comets are a thing of the past, I assure you."

Frederica longed to say, "And Clarissa?" but the kiss was a small victory and with that she had to be content.

The Countess's villa in the King's Road was cold. The female guests were arrayed in light fluttering muslins and lawns and acres of gooseflesh. Some of the more daring had damped their muslins and shivered as they undulated around the draughty conservatory at the back of the villa. Frederica was heartily glad of the latest modish addition to her wardrobe — a pair of knickers.

Archie Hefford claimed Frederica's hand for the first dance and she left her husband's side with a little pang of regret.

When the dance finished, she found Clarissa at her side, a vision of loveliness in aquamarine muslin with little blue artificial forget-me-nots twined in her golden hair. She waved her spangled fan languidly in the direction of the Duke who was talking to Emily. "So glad Henry decided to take my advice and attend," she murmured. "He told me that you had planned a little *soiree* at home but I said 'My dear Henry, all the world and his wife will be there. You must come.' And he said in that funny way of his, 'But will you be there?' and when I said I would, he replied, 'Nothing will keep me away!' "

Her large blue eyes slid sideways to see the effect of her words on Frederica. The girl looked positively stricken.

Frederica was remembering Henry's guilty look when he had explained that they must go. He had said the Countess had been particularly expecting them, but the Countess had not paid them any special attention.

The Duke was laughing at something

Emily said. Clarissa left Frederica's side and went forward to join them. Frederica moved off into the dance with her next partner, moving like a clockwork toy. Her partner was Jack Ferrand. He noticed the start of surprise she gave and the look of distaste which followed when she realized who her partner was. He set himself to please but with the intricate steps of the country dance, he was afforded little opportunity.

It was the first ball Frederica had attended for some time and she was never short of partners. The Duke looked on, at first with tolerant amusement, and then with slowly growing anger as he began to understand that she was avoiding him. Abruptly, he turned to Archie Hefford at his side. "I have remembered another engagement," he said, "please convey my apologies to my wife. Can you escort her home?" As Archie nodded, Jack Ferrand who had been listening to the conversation, slipped off and went in search of Clarissa. "You must disappear at the same time," he told her. "Then Frederica will think that you have left together. Leave me to arrange things with Mrs. Sayers."

"But I don't want to go," pouted Clarissa.

"Go," he said calmly, "or take the consequences."

Fretting under his re-established authority, Clarissa moved quickly from the ballroom and after the disappearing Duke.

"Henry," she called after him. "Please take me home. I think I have caught a cold."

He turned round and surveyed her with weary boredom. "Where is your mother?"

"Oh, mama has elected to stay. That is, if you will give me your escort. There is, after all, nothing unconventional about accepting the escort of one's brother-in-law."

He nodded his head wearily and led her out to his carriage. He could not help thinking that a short time ago it would have meant the world and all to be alone with her. He cursed his wife under his breath. Clarissa deftly laid little pieces of gossip on his anger to fan the flame. Had he noticed how prodigious popular Frederica had become with the gentlemen? And then with a stroke of daring, she said she had taken Frederica to task for having so many admirers. To which he replied through clenched teeth, "And what did she reply?"

"Oh, you know Frederica," said Clarissa airily, "she just laughed and said she had a very modern marriage."

For the first time, the Duke began seriously to consider his wife in a new light. All her innocence and blushes now appeared to be the manners of a designing minx.

It was only after he had set Clarissa down in Clarence Square that he remembered the long days that Frederica had spent alone in the library. He remembered also Clarissa's patent dislike and envy of her stepsister in the early days, and felt a small pang of guilt. He decided to wait up for her.

But Frederica, with her feet as sore as her heart, from determinedly dancing all through the night, did not return until six the following morning, by which time the Duke was fast asleep in the library.

Determined to have things out with him, Frederica marched to his bedroom to find it empty and unslept in.

She was too hurt and angry to cry. Her handsome husband would find no further opportunities to break her heart. She had enough cards and invitations to keep herself fully occupied. It was a marriage of convenience. No more. And the sooner she began to treat it as such, the better.

The Duke woke late in the morning, stiff and sore from sleeping in the armchair and went in search of his wife only to be informed that she had gone out shopping.

He decided to immerse himself in work, ordered his bags to be packed, and departed for Chartsay.

As the weeks passed, the only news he received from London was in the form of various notes from Clarissa coyly teasing him over his wife's "racketing around."

At last, he posted up to town with the intention of bringing his erring wife home to Chartsay for Christmas only to find that she had already left for the Hefford's country home in Hertforshire.

For the first time, he seriously began to consider a divorce.

Chapter Eleven

Hagglestone Hall, home of the Heffords, was a large square mansion which had been designed by Sanderson Miller in the middle of the last century. It was unprepossessing from the outside, having no portico or grand entrance, but as Archie pointed out it was an essentially English house and "looked very well in the rain."

What it lacked in grandeur on the outside was compensated by the richness and elegance of the apartments on the inside. Sensibly planned, the main rooms on the ground floor led into each other on a sort of circuit plan. It was possible to reach the downstairs by a fairly direct route from one's bedroom instead of wandering helplessly up and down a labyrinth of stairs and passages as one did in some of the older mansions.

Archie had planned to celebrate Christmas in the Hanoverian manner. The gallery was decorated like a fairground with a table at one end for Archie's gifts to his friends and a table at the other for the guests' gifts to Archie. In the middle stood an enormous Christmas tree loaded with oranges, sweetmeats and gingerbread. Archie had decided to let the tenants' children loose on the tree on Christmas morn.

Emily was alternately worried about her "platter-faced" friend, Priscilla Wheatcroft, and the marriage of her other friend, Frederica.

For Frederica would discuss her marriage with no one, and Priscilla collapsed into noisy tears every time the gentlemen went out shooting, bemoaning the fate of the "dear birdies." None of Emily's bracing remarks that her friend's concern over the fate of the "dear birdies" did not extend to the dining table where Priscilla had consumed almost one whole duck the night before did anything to stop her mourning.

Stafford's interpretation to Mrs. Cholmley that Priscilla "yea, was beating her breast in sore distress over the slaughter in the land" did little to help. It simply made the other guests laugh hilariously at the unfortunate Priscilla who looked in a fair way to become the joke of the Christmas season.

Frederica was lonely and Jack Ferrand sensed it. He put himself out to be so agreeable that she almost forgot her mistrust of him. He introduced her to the delights of

gambling and praised her skill extravagantly. Frederica began to look forward to
the card tables in the long winter evenings
where she could forget her sorrows in the
skill of the game. Archie teased her about
her gambling and said she was trying to
compete with the Prince Regent who was
having trouble in Parliament over his Civil
List, being more than £300,000 in debt.

But Frederica was unconcerned. They
were playing for pennies after all.

The arrival of Mr. Pellington-James was a
welcome diversion. He shared Priscilla
Wheatcroft's dislike of blood sports, which
should have thrown them into each other's
company, but Chuffy had so long been in
the bachelor habit of paying court to unob-
tainable beauties that he did not know how
to go on with an available girl and avoided
her as much as he could, much to Archie's
disappointment.

On Christmas Eve, Archie announced
they would have a skating party since the
lake had frozen solid. Lanterns were
threaded through the skeletal winter trees at
the edge of the ice, their myriad colors setting the frosty landscape sparkling and
flashing like diamonds. It was a romantic
setting and Frederica as she glided inex-
pertly on Jack Ferrand's arm, could not but

wish that her husband had decided to join them. She had sent him a gift of a Sevres snuff box from Gray's and kept looking at the presents in the long gallery in the hope that he had sent her something in return to show that he still remembered that he had a wife.

She saw the forlorn figure of Priscilla standing at the edge of the ice and called to Jack Ferrand to halt. "I am sure Miss Wheatcroft would enjoy a turn on the ice, Mr. Ferrand," she cried.

Jack Ferrand surveyed the trembling figure of Miss Wheatcroft with dislike. She was dressed in an extremely smart skating rig of scarlet velvet with gold frogs but her long nose was just as red and her thin sandy hair poked out in wisps from her under bonnet. With a sigh of relief he spotted the approaching bulk of Chuffy.

"Ah, Chuffy," he cried. "There is a vastly pretty lady waiting for your escort!" Priscilla turned around with a radiant smile on her face but Chuffy lumbered straight past her and took Frederica's arm. "Delighted to oblige," he said, gliding off with Frederica.

There was nothing else Jack Ferrand could do but escort Priscilla. Then he noticed the jealous and venomous glance Miss

Wheatcroft threw in Frederica's direction and felt more charitably inclined towards the girl. She could yet be useful.

"Where is our dear Duchess' husband?" said Priscilla, following Frederica's slim figure with a wintry look that sparkled like the frost-covered fields.

"He is at Chartsay," replied Jack Ferrand, neatly executing an intricate turn. He lowered his voice, "May I tell you something in strict confidence?"

"But of course!" breathed Priscilla, her long nose twitching like a rabbit.

"It is said that the Duke seeks a divorce."

Priscilla put her gloved hand to her mouth and gave a delighted "Oh!" and her fervent assurances that the news would go no further. She then glided off to spread the delicious tidbit round the other guests as soon as she could. She was clever enough to keep the news from Emily, however. Even Priscilla knew that her dear friend was positively "blinded with affection" when it came to matters concerning the Duchess.

Jack Ferrand looked on with delight as Miss Wheatcroft sped from group to group over the lake, glad to have people stop and listen to her at last. Mr. Ferrand reflected on the ways of the world and considered it was simply marvellous that no one would consider telling Frederica what was being said about herself.

Frederica became uncomfortably aware of whispers and pitying glances and suddenly wished that the card tables could be set up so that she could lose herself in the game.

A thaw set in on Christmas morning with a great gusty wind driving sheets of rain against the window panes. A parcel arrived for the Duchess of Westerland and she tore open the wrapping with shaking fingers. It was a pretty gold filigree bracelet which she tossed aside while she searched for a note. With trembling fingers she opened the thin slip of paper and read the spidery handwriting. It said, "His Grace, the Duke of Westerland, presents his compliments to Her Grace, the Duchess of Westerland with many wishes for a pleasant Christmas." The note was signed. "Your humble and obedient servant, James Entwhistle, secretary."

The most recent addition to the Duke's household, secretary James Entwhistle, could never have guessed what agonies his simple note had caused.

Frederica's misery was complete. The noisy Christmas festivities washed passed her as she stood on a little rocky island of loneliness and despair. Only in the intricacies of piquet or whist did she manage to escape from her tortured thoughts.

She took her new-found gambling fever back to the empty rooms of Grosvenor Square with her but, to Jack Ferrand's eternal disappointment, she drew the line at visiting gambling clubs, however select. The stakes were too high, she protested, and it was not her own money to lose. She contented herself with ladylike games of whist or silver loo when the card tables were set up after dinner in the households of her friends.

The quiet Miss Wheatcroft had been busy and it eventually came to Emily's ears that her dear friend had been gossiping about Frederica's supposed impending divorce around every salon and drawing room in London.

In a towering rage, she sent Priscilla packing and then rushed round to Grosvenor Square and asked Frederica bluntly if the news were true. "*I* am not considering a divorce," said Frederica. "It must mean that it is your brother who is considering it."

"Then it's a piece of idle gossip," snapped Emily. "If, by any chance, Henry were considering a divorce he would certainly not tell anyone. He never discusses his marriage. I am one of the few who know it was a marriage of convenience and the two of you seem to have been rubbing along tolerably well. It's not as if either of you were in the habit of having lovers' quarrels!"

Perhaps if Emily had not been so robust and matter-of-fact, Frederica might have confided in her. But she had received so many hurts and humiliations since her marriage that she cringed from another rebuff. Emily might point out that she should never have married brother Henry unless she was willing to meet the terms of the marriage.

Frederica plunged once more into the social round and, when her husband returned to town, she found herself accepting as many as four or five invitations a day. The Duke returned to his Corinthian sports of boxing, curricle racing, and other manly pursuits and spent most of his evenings in either White's, Watier's, or Brooks.

Priscilla's one piece of gossip died as the ducal couple continued to share the same roof and more tantalizing *on-dits* began to circulate.

Frederica felt as if she had never led such a dissipated life but to Jack Ferrand's jaundiced eyes, she seemed the model of propriety.

He decided to call on Clarissa.

To his surprise, he was informed that Miss Sayers was not at home although he could hear her laugh echoing from the drawing room.

He returned to his carriage outside the house in Clarence Square and waited patiently. Half an hour later, the thin mincing figure of Lord Adderson descended the stairs. Lord Adderson was a young widower who had reportedly run through his own fortune, his late wife's fortune, and was now said to be on the look-out for another.

Jack Ferrand waited until Lord Adderson's carriage had turned the corner of the square and then mounted the house steps again. He pushed past the startled butler and strode into the drawing room. Clarissa and her mother were in a great flutter about something and both of them turned and stared at him with haughty displeasure.

"A word with you in private, Miss Sayers," said Jack, holding open the door for Mrs. Sayers who started to bridle and protest but was cut short rudely by Clarissa.

"Go on, mama. I am quite capable of dealing with this . . . gentleman."

Both waited in silence until Mrs. Sayers had left. "I gather you are to be congratulated," said Jack Ferrand.

"Yes," yawned Clarissa, waving her fan languidly to and fro.

"Then my girl, let me remind you that the marriage will never take place if you continue to give me such cavalier treatment."

"Do your worst," mocked Clarissa. "Percy Adderson will never believe you. He is much too interested in my fortune."

"He may not, but the rest of London society will. And Adderson has a grim mama and a very old name to protect. You would never get near the altar."

Clarissa turned white and dropped her fan. "You wouldn't dare."

"You know I would," he said. "You have only one more little thing to do for me. You will go to the Duke all concern for your little sister. You will tell him that Frederica has been keeping low company and is in the habit of frequenting a certain Mrs. O'Brien's establishment. You will say as a clincher that she is to be there tonight. And you will leave the rest to me."

"You are too cruel," Clarissa sobbed. "*I* am tired of this whole matter."

"Don't waste your tears on me," he said brutally. "I am not one of your gallants. You will do this one last thing or you will never be Lady Adderson."

She did not reply but stared at him white-faced through her tears.

"Answer me," he commanded, twisting her arm behind her back.

"Yes . . . yes," whispered Clarissa. "But, by God, I hate you more than any other vermin on the face of this earth."

"Just do it," he said, releasing her. "Here is Mrs. O'Brien's direction. Go to the Duke this morning."

Clarissa watched him stride from the room through a mist of tears. She decided to call on her brother-in-law while she was still distressed and frightened. Henry had an uncomfortably shrewd eye.

"If ever I get out of this coil," she swore to herself, "Frederica can marry the Prince Regent for all I care!" It suddenly struck her that this was at least a somewhat unselfish thought and she felt strangely comforted.

She was leaving to collect her cloak and bonnet when she almost collided with Mrs. Sayers. "Sit down for a minute, Clarissa," said her mama with unwonted severity. "Are you going to throw your engagement to Adderson to the winds by receiving that man, Ferrand, unchaperoned?"

"Why, mama, he is an old friend!"

"A young unmarried man who whispers in corners with a young unmarried girl is no friend," said Mrs. Sayers grimly. "What is behind these meetings? Out with it!"

For a split second, Clarissa thought furiously, then she forced a smile. "Why, mama. I was sure you would have guessed. It was Mr. Ferrand who fostered my engagement to Lord Adderson."

"Indeed!" cried Mrs. Sayers, much mollified. "Then we are very much beholden to him. Lord! I'd love to see Frederica's face when she hears you are marrying a title."

Clarissa looked at her mother in some surprise. Could not Mrs. Sayers understand her stepdaughter enough to know that Frederica would not care one way or the other?

"You know, mama," remarked Clarissa in a conversational voice, "you are a remarkably stupid woman."

"How dare you!" gasped Mrs. Sayers and mother and daughter fell into one of their tormenting, harrying and chivvying arguments with all the enthusiasm of old campaigners.

They went at it hammer and tongs for nigh on an hour until Clarissa, who was just about to throw one of her famous tantrums to somehow clinch the argument of her mother's stupidity, recollected her appointment and left a startled Mrs. Sayers in mid-scream.

The Duke had not yet left for his club. Clarissa was ushered into the Egyptian room and left to await him. A cheerful fire was crackling on the hearth, sending little sparkles of light glinting from the glass sphinxes' heads on the pilasters of the fireplace. The Duchess was fortunately absent. Through the long windows, she could see glimpses of the leaden sky outside. Her mission began to take on an air of unreality and Clarissa fervently wished that she could simply get up and go away and forget about the whole thing.

The door opened and the Duke entered. He was dressed to go out in a blue fitted swallowtail coat, striped waistcoat, buckskins, and polished hessians. He had lost his tan and his thin, white handsome face looked unwontedly severe. To Clarissa, he seemed like a formidable opponent. Her nerves and distress returned and she began to cry most convincingly. Despite her very obvious distress, the Duke experienced nothing more than a pang of boredom until through her sobs, he caught the mention of his wife's name.

Three quick strides took him to her side and he jerked her to her feet. "Frederica! What about Frederica?" he demanded, holding the sobbing girl by the shoulders and resisting an impulse to shake her hard.

With an effort, Clarissa pulled herself together. She may as well get it over quickly.

"Poor F-Frederica," she stammered, holding a wisp of handkerchief to her eyes. "She has got into bad habits and bad company and spends her nights g-gambling in low dives."

The Duke released her. "Fustian," he remarked coldly.

Clarissa was suddenly terrified that he would not believe her. "It's true," she cried. "Why I know that tonight you will be able to find her at her usual rendezvous, a Mrs. O'Brien's."

"Mrs. O'Brien's. Come, come. Do you take me for a flat? My wife may not yet be up to all the ways of the world. But she certainly would not attend a gambling hell frequented by card sharps and the demimonde."

"But it's true!" wailed Clarissa, almost believing it herself in her desperation.

The Duke sat down and crossed one muscular leg over the other and surveyed her coldly. "It occurs to me that if Frederica were disgracing herself by frequenting a low establishment it would surely be a source of joy to you rather than otherwise. You can act very coyly and prettily, my girl, but I am persuaded that there is not one whit of truth in all this farradiddle. Why this sudden concern for Frederica's welfare?"

Clarissa played her trump card. She opened her beautiful eyes and gave him a direct look. "I see I cannot fool you, Henry. The fact is I have become engaged to Lord Adderson this very morn. Any breath of scandal attached to our name and . . ."

She did not need to finish. The Duke vividly recalled her desire for a title. He leaned forward. "I shall go to Mrs. O'Brien's tonight. If Frederica is there, God help her. An' she is not . . . then God help you, dear Clarissa."

Clarissa recoiled. The Duke's eyes were blazing and she realized with a thrill of terror that he was likely to be a much more formidable enemy than Jack Ferrand. She had a sudden impulse to tell him the truth but he had risen to his feet and rung the bell for the servant to show her out.

She almost ran from the house to her carriage and nearly collided with a small female figure who was lurking on the pavement.

"Why! Miss Wheatcroft," exclaimed Clarissa recognising the foxy face peeping out from a poke bonnet. "What are you doing here?"

"I have urgent news for Mr. Pellington-James," whispered Priscilla, the tip of her nose twitching in an irritating manner. "Do you have his direction?"

"He has lodgings in Albemarle Street, I believe," said Clarissa coldly. "I suggest you go there and enquire."

The little figure scuttled off leaving Clarissa to stare after her. What was that all about? Clarissa had a comforting feeling that at least Chuffy was in for as bad a morning as she was experiencing herself.

A new Chuffy Pellington-James was at that moment ambling in a leisurely manner back to his flat in Albemarle Street. Overcome by the friendship of such a notable Corinthian as the Duke of Westerland, and tired of the malice of the Dandy set, Chuffy had decided to adopt the Corinthian mode.

He had just visited his tailors, Weston and Meyer in Conduit Street, to supervise the structure of a suit of evening clothes that even Mr. Brummell would find unexceptionable. Rigid days of sports and exercise had reduced his stomach to comfortable proportions and his rosy face, free of its customary white paint, beamed on the world.

Even a rigidly starched cravat tied in the Oriental failed to mar Chuffy's comfort.

Free of stays and high heels, he felt like a new man.

He was cheerfully whistling "The Girl I Left Behind Me" and looking forward to changing his clothes and having a well-earned lunch at his club, when the whistle died on his lips. He found himself looking down at the unforgettable face of Priscilla Wheatcroft who was clutching the railings at the entrance to his flag.

"Oh, Mr. Pellington-James," she gasped weakly. "Thank goodness it is you. I am feeling faint. Do you think you could procure me a glass of water?"

"Well, no I can't," said Chuffy baldly. "M'man's got the day off. 'Sides it wouldn't be the thing to have a lady in my flat. Where's your maid?"

"She . . . she fell ill too," whispered Priscilla, swaying against the railings.

Chuffy swore under his breath and looked quickly up and down the street. No one was in sight. "You can come in for a minute," he said. "And make sure nobody sees you leavin'."

She nodded and clung onto his arm. Together they climbed the stairs to his second-floor apartments. He fumbled for his key and let her in to a dark hallway. "What an interesting *little* key," cried Priscilla, holding out her hand. "May I see it?"

He handed it to her. "It's the latest Chubb lock," he said proudly. "No felon's going to pick that one."

"Really," exclaimed Priscilla, inserting the key in the inside lock. "And when I turn it like this, there you are, all locked in, safe and sound."

"Well . . . er . . . yes," said Chuffy, holding out his hand for the key but she moved in front of him into his small book-lined parlor.

Before Chuffy knew what she was about she had run to the window which was open a few inches at the bottom and hurled the key out into the street.

"What the . . ." began Chuffy.

She turned and faced him with her back to the window, a smile of triumph curving her thin lips. "You are *compromised,* Mr. Pellington-James," she cried. "Now you will need to marry me!"

Chuffy moved quickly to the window. The street looked a very long way down. "I could scream for help," he remarked.

She gave a scornful laugh. "A large man like you, screaming for help! Why, you would be the laughing stock of London."

Gloomily, Chuffy realized this to be true. The new respect and compliments he had earned since he had joined the Corinthian set were not to be thrown away lightly. He sat down suddenly and surveyed Priscilla Wheatcroft with a drawn, hard look beginning to form on his usually cheerful features.

He began to pull off his boots.

"Why, Mr. Pellington-James! What are you doing?" screamed Priscilla.

"Makin' the most of it," said Chuffy laconically, removing his jacket.

"But . . . this is not what I planned," stammered Priscilla.

Chuffy tore off his cravat and removed his splendid waistcoat.

"I shall scream for help," said Priscilla, breathing hard.

Chuffy removed his shirt and then his undervest. "Won't do you any good," he remarked cheerfully. "Nobody in the house and the window won't open any further."

He hitched a thumb into the top of his trousers and looked across at Miss Wheatcroft who was staring at his naked hairy chest and looking now as if she was really going to faint.

He approached her slowly as she backed into a corner of the room. "You said I was compromised, Miss Wheatcroft," he said with a wicked gleam in his eye. "But you're the one that's going to be compromised so you may as well make the best of it. Come here to me."

Like a rabbit hypnotized by a snake, Priscilla moved slowly towards him. He caught her round the waist and removed her bonnet and threw it on the sofa.

"Why!" he exclaimed. "It's beginning to snow. How cosy."

But Miss Priscilla Wheatcroft only let out a faint moan. Things were not going the way she had planned during her long journey to town from the country. Things were certainly not going her way one little bit.

As Frederica's carriage turned into Grosvenor Square, she was just in time to see her husband's smart yellow curricle bowling out of the other end. She gave a little sigh. It was just as well. Confrontations were painful. When they met, he treated her with a chilling formality. He was absent most nights, not returning till the small hours. Frederica often heard him enter as she tossed and turned on her pillow, unable to sleep until she knew he was home. A fine, light snow was beginning to fall from the leaden sky. She was bone weary from the hectic round of social engagements, always hoping by some miracle that her husband would attend one of them and smile on her. But when he did attend, he afforded her no more than a common bow and promptly retired to the card room. Frederica did not know how bitterly he loathed her crowd of gallants and how desperately he wished he could snatch her from them.

She felt immeasurably weary in body and spirit as she walked into the hall. Worthing, the butler, presented her with a note folded in the shape of a cocked hat.

"This arrived for you this morning, Your Grace," he said.

Frederica removed her bonnet and cloak and handed them to Worthing and then opened the note. The writing seemed to leap out of the page at her.

"If you wish to know where your husband spends his evenings — and with whom — pay a visit tonight to Mrs. O'Brien's gambling house, 128 Cork Street."

It was unsigned. Frederica rounded on Worthing. "Who brought this?"

"A footman, Your Grace. He was in plain livery and I do not know from which household he came."

"Very good, Worthing," said Frederica faintly. "That will be all."

She crumpled the note in her hand and stared into space. She would not go. She would not be confronted by her husband's latest lightskirt.

But then the thought of this agonizing marriage dragging its painful weary way on through the winter's days was too much. She had to know the worst. Confronted by her in such a place, he must surely come to a decision — divorce . . . or rearrange the marriage to more comfortable terms.

The weary day dragged on as the steadily falling snow transformed London into a black and white etching, dancing, twirling, and falling in the pale flickering light of the parish lamps.

Frederica dined alone in her rooms and then rang for her maid. Dressed in a gown of white merino with silver stripes and a red velvet cloak lined with ermine, she trailed slowly down the stairs to come face to face with her husband who was also dressed in evening clothes.

"May I escort you somewhere, my lady?" he asked in a thin cold voice.

"N-no," stammered Frederica. "I mean do not trouble. I am going to Emily's and I am sure that it is out of your way."

The Duke regarded his little wife speculatively. "I had forgotten, of course, that you prefer other escorts. Go on your way, madame." He turned on his heel and walked off into his study and left her standing alone in the large hall.

Frederica half turned and made as though to run after him. But the study door shut behind him with a loud bang.

As she climbed into her carriage, a little of the fear began to leave her. Of course, it was all a hum! How could he be going to a gambling hell when she had left him at home. She would pay a call on Emily after all, and then just look in at Mrs. O'Brien's.

She had taken the precaution of ordering the services of two burly footmen to accompany her. There would be no danger of a reenactment of the Barnet episode.

There was still enough of the child in Frederica to enjoy the sparkling snow despite her apprehension. And Emily always gave her a warm welcome.

Mrs. O'Brien's indeed! He would probably go to his club.

Chapter Twelve

The gambling hell did not present a very sinister appearance from the outside. A neat brick fronted, three-storied building with white painted window sashes and a glossy white door with a well-polished knocker, it did not seem to Frederica to be the type of mansion she had associated with the demimonde.

But telling the two footmen to accompany her, she picked her way up the steps, which had been freshly cleared of snow.

Mrs. O'Brien put one large eye to the crack in the curtain and swivelled it round to follow Frederica's slight figure as she mounted the steps outside followed by her footmen.

"A crest, no less," she murmured, surveying the coach. "Some lord has sent his mistress along in fine style."

"That, dear Mrs. O'Brien, is no mistress. That is none other than the Duchess of Westerland."

"Lud!" Mrs. O'Brien swung her massive figure round and surveyed Jack Ferrand over her several chins. "What does Her Grace want frequenting a place like this?"

"You underrate the charms of your establishment," he said smoothly. "Do not be put off by the Duchess's youthful appearance and innocent air. She is a dedicated gambler."

"So? There are fancy establishments enough in Mayfair to cater to the likes of her."

"The Duchess," Jack Ferrand went on, "has a certain little-known penchant for wild young men. Her husband is very strict so she cannot satisfy her . . . er needs in her immediate circle. She is also exceedingly wealthy!"

"Oho! Then since she knows what she's about, it's up to me to supply such a plump little chicken with what she desires."

Mrs. O'Brien moved rapidly among the tables, stopping here and there to speak with certain young men. With a snap of her fingers, a new table was set up just as Frederica made her entrance.

Mrs. O'Brien cruised majestically forward, enveloping Frederica in an air of false bonhommie.

Jack Ferrand had disappeared from view. Mrs. O'Brien sank into a low curtsy and then wheezed to her feet with great difficulty. "A great honor, Your Grace," she panted. "Please come this way."

Frederica decided against mentioning her husband. He was obviously not in the room. She would play one game and then make her departure.

As she followed Mrs. O'Brien, she looked around nervously. Everyone seemed to have stopped playing in order to stare at her. Many of the women wore necklines so low that the tops of their nipples showed and their transparent dresses had been damped to show as much of their form as they indecently could.

"Here we are," said Mrs. O'Brien jovially pulling out a chair for Frederica. There were five young bucks at the table, all the worse for wine, and all sprawled at their ease.

"I do not care to join this company," Frederica started to say when things began to move very quickly.

One of the young bucks pulled Frederica down onto his knee and she sprawled across him while his friends roared and cheered. Mrs. O'Brien knew from the look on Frederica's face that a dreadful mistake had been made. She made a move to help Frederica but a commotion in the doorway made her swing round.

The Duke of Westerland stood there, his grey eyes like flat pieces of slate in his white face. The whole room froze. Mrs. O'Brien had one hand stretched towards Frederica and the other towards the Duke. Frederica's skirt was rucked up as far as her garters and the Duke was to remember long afterwards that the thing that made his temper snap was the fact that this was the first time he had so much as seen his wife's legs and it had to be in the middle of a gambling hell under the painted eyelids of half the demi-monde.

He bounded forward and delivered a smashing left straight into the face of the buck who was holding Frederica. Then with one arm he jerked her to her feet like a rag doll.

To Frederica, it was like a nightmare. She opened her mouth but no sound came. She was unceremoniously dragged from the room and bundled into her cloak, then dragged again out into the snow.

That little scene was burned into Frederica's mind like a brand for long afterwards — the Duke with his white face and glittering eyes, Mrs. O'Brien's great bosoms spilling over the window ledge of the club as she stared at them, the smell of whale oil from the parish lamp above her head mixing with the smells of wine, cigars and patchouli emanating from the club, and finally, the feel of the feathery snow on her face and the feel of the damp snow underfoot seeping through her thin slippers. The Duke said: "You will be removed from London to Chartsay immediately until I present suitable grounds for divorce. The servants at Chartsay will be informed that you are not to leave the grounds for any reason whatever. I wish I had never married you, madame. I most certainly never want to set eyes on you again."

Frederica found her voice too late. With an imperious wave of his hand, he hailed a passing hackney cabriolet and disappeared into the snow.

Frederica knew that it was useless to plead with the servants. Her husband was lord and master. They would not listen to a word that she said.

Even Worthing was meticulously correct as to the arranging and dispatching of her trunks. Only her maid, the stern Benson, broke down and cried as she shared her mistress's disgrace. Frederica was not even going to be allowed to wait for morning. As soon as she had changed into her travelling dress, the coach was waiting outside with her trunks corded on the back and the horses of the outriders stamping and snuffling in the snow.

The coach rumbled off. She thought of Lawton, the Groom of the Chambers at Chartsay, and a picture of his fat white face seemed to swim in front of her eyes and she shuddered.

Pride had stopped her from writing an explanation to her husband. He had not trusted her. And in any case, she could not have produced the letter that had lured her to the club because, when she had searched in her reticule for it, it was gone.

A livid dawn spread over snow-covered London as Mrs. O'Brien waddled round the now-empty gaming room snuffing out the candles. She stood on tiptoe, reaching up with the brass snuffer to the last and tallest of the candles without success. She looked round for a chair to stand on and saw a piece of crumpled paper on the floor. Wheezing for breath she bent over to pick it up.

Never leave a piece of paper lying, she thought — it might always be an I.O.U. She smoothed out the parchment with her swollen and mottled fingers and then carried it over to the light of the one remaining candle. She read "If you wish to know where your husband spends his evenings — and with whom — pay a visit tonight to Mrs. O'Brien's gambling house, 128 Cork Street."

She shook her turbaned head over it. It must have something to do with the Duchess for the note had been lying by her chair. And why had Jack Ferrand misled her? Somewhere and somehow the two were connected and somewhere and somehow there might be money in it for Mrs. O'Brien. But she was too old and too weary to cope with the problem at that moment. Standing on a chair, she snuffed the last wavering candle and waddled off to bed as the pale dawn changed to blood red, turning the snow colored streets to crimson. For a few brief moments, the glare illuminated the empty gambling room with a hellish glow, fading to grey and then black as the snow began to fall and the dreary clang-clang of the watchman's bell sounded down the early morning streets.

The same brief crimson glow awoke Frederica from a fitful sleep. She was chilled and cramped. The carriage swung into the long drive leading to Chartsay and as they approached the great house, the red glow faded, leaving the towers and battlements silhouetted against the heavy black sky.

Lawton, complete with cane emerged onto the entrance steps to meet the carriage. He made Frederica a low bow and pasted a smile on his unlovely features. One of the footmen who had travelled with Frederica presented Lawton with a letter with the instructions that he was to read it immediately.

Frederica moved slowly across the great chilly hall towards her apartments. "Have tea brought to my rooms, Lawton," she called over her shoulder.

Something in the quality of the silence made her turn round. Lawton was looking straight at her. He had just finished reading the letter with the Duke's instructions and his face was twisted with malevolent glee. "I am afraid that will not be possible, Your Grace," he said with a mock bow. "The servants are still abed."

Frederica was too fatigued to argue. She turned her back on him and went to her rooms.

She slept heavily for three hours and awoke hungry despite her misery. She rang the bell and waited . . . and waited. Growing impatient, she sent Benson to see what was up with the servants. Benson bustled back after quarter of an hour, her mouth in a thin furious line.

"That fat slug, Lawton," she cried. "He says the staff are all too busy to attend to your needs. I told him that the Duke would hear of his behavior and he said . . . he said . . ." here Benson burst into tears. "Oh, ma'am," she sobbed, "he says the Duke won't care what becomes of you." Frederica's face was as white as the powdery snow drifting and eddying on the terrace outside.

"He means to starve us," said Frederica in a flat voice. "The steward, Benjamin Dubble, where is he?"

"In London seeing the Duke," faltered Benson. "Oh what on earth are we to do?"

Frederica suddenly gritted her teeth. She was not going to spend the rest of her life being bullied. Mrs. Sayers had been enough. She got to her feet. "You'll see, Benson. You'll see!"

The terrified and sobbing maid followed close behind her young mistress who stalked out into the hall and up to the first landing of the grand staircase. Frederica seized the rope of the fire alarm and gave it a mighty pull. The clang-clang-clanging echoed through the great house and soon there were loud cries of fire and figures scurrying to and fro in the hallway. One by one, as they looked up to see who had been ringing the fire bell, they saw the small figure of the Duchess, standing on the landing, clutching the balustrade and looking down into the hall. One by one they fell silent. One by one they stopped. Frederica waited until she guessed that practically all the servants were gathered in the hall. Lawton looked insolently amused, some of the footmen sniggered, but the rest waited in silence.

Frederica's voice was as chill and cold as the musty air in the hall.

"You have all, as far as I know," she began, "been guilty of the most insolent and disloyal behavior. Whatever the situation between myself and my husband may be I think you should know him well enough to know that he would not tolerate such treatment of his wife."

Lawton merely grinned and gave a fat wink to his sister who smiled back.

"I am sure however that there are some amongst you who realize the enormity of your behavior. If there are any among you who would serve me as befits my rank and as the Duke would wish, stand to one side. I would know my friends."

There was a long silence. Benson thought that no one was going to move. Then amid jeers and cat calls, the small knife boy walked to one side of the hall and stood with his hands behind his back looking up at Frederica. Then the under butler, a man named Bond, moved to join him. He was slowly followed by several housemaids and six of the footmen. The smile began to leave Lawton's face. The still-room maid suddenly scampered to join Frederica's side. A pretty, mischievous-looking girl with a mop of fair curls, she seemed a general favorite.

Several more followed after her, including the two footmen from the Grosvenor Square household who had travelled down with Frederica.

When the ranks were divided and no more moved to Frederica's side of the hall, she spoke again. "All those loyal to me will be rewarded. The rest of you will lose your jobs as soon as my husband hears of this affair. Furthermore . . ."

She broke off as the great doors burst open and the rector and his wife stood on the threshold. Mrs. Witherspoon ran forward and then stopped in amazement at the rows of divided servants, the grinning Lawton, and the small stern figure of the Duchess.

"My dear Duchess, what is the meaning of this?" cried Mrs. Witherspoon.

"Mutiny in the ranks," shouted Frederica with a grin of relief.

Mrs. Witherspoon wheeled about, "This is all your doing, Lawton, you great fat *useless* man." And before Lawton realized her intent, Mrs. Witherspoon had set about him with her red silk umbrella, beating him resoundingly about the head and shoulders until she was pulled away by her startled husband.

While the rector was explaining that they had heard the sound of the bell and rushed to help, Mrs. Witherspoon rounded on the rest of the servants.

"Leave and go about your duties, all of you," shouted Mrs. Witherspoon. One by one they sheepishly filed out, those that had elected to be loyal to Lawton feeling as if they had just made a dreadful mistake.

Frederica ran lightly down the stairs and fell half weeping, half laughing into Mrs. Witherspoon's motherly arms.

When breakfast had finally been served by the under butler, Frederica found herself pouring out all her troubles into Mrs. Witherspoon's sympathetic ear. It was such a relief to talk to someone that she felt she would never stop. The rector had tactfully taken himself off to the library. When Frederica finally finished, Mrs. Witherspoon leaned back in her chair and surveyed her with amazement. "Marriage of convenience, be damned," she cried and then was glad her husband was not around to hear her lapse. "It seems to me as if you two ninnyhammers are head over heels in love and don't know it. And pride, my dear. Such pride! Not to tell your husband of your terrible experience in Barnet and to think poor Henry had anything to do with it is beyond belief."

Frederica sighed. "You make it all sound so simple. But it was not like that at the time. If the Comte were to be believed then *someone* was trying to harm me and still is. And . . . and I believe Henry is still in love with Clarissa."

"Pooh!" said Mrs. Witherspoon. "He does not look at Clarissa the way he looks at you."

"Me?" faltered Frederica.

"Yes, you. I think his eyes were opened to Clarissa a long time ago. I think you will find that he only suffers her company because she is your sister."

"What am I to do?" begged Frederica.

"Wait until the roads are clear," said Mrs. Witherspoon, "and give me a letter and I shall have the rectory boy sent to London with it. Explain everything to your husband. Leave nothing out . . . including your love for him. It will be all right, you'll see. One of you has to break down these barriers of hurt pride and I am afraid, my dear that in this present world that that is usually the lot of the female.

"Why, even now, the Duke will have realized his dreadful mistake!"

But the Duke had not, although he was becoming increasingly worried. He had just returned to Grosvenor Square after a distressing meeting with his sister, Emily, and her fiance, Archie Hefford. Both had been shocked at Frederica's behavior but Emily insisted there must have been something behind it.

"She came here to see me that evening," said Emily. "And she was very upset and nervous and near to tears. She would not tell me what was the matter or where she was going. She simply kept repeating that she had a pressing engagement."

Even Aunt Matilda Cholmley had waved aside Stafford's "yea verily" translations to remark abruptly. "That gel's in love with you, Henry."

All looked at her in surprise but after that one sentence, Aunt Matilda had retreated back into her silent world and would say no more.

The Duke was pacing up and down in his study when Mr. Pellington-James was announced.

Chuffy had dark circles round his eyes but looked remarkably like a large cat that had just swallowed a particularly delicious canary.

"I've got tremendous news," he cried cheerfully. "Where's Frederica?"

"My wife is at the moment resident in the country where she will remain for some time," remarked the Duke stonily.

Chuffy's large face fell. "What a disappointment. She would be so thrilled at my news." He looked hopefully at the Duke who was still pacing up and down and then asked plaintively, "Well, ain't you even goin' to *ask* me what my news is?"

The Duke stopped his pacing and regarded him with some irritation, "Oh, very well. What *is* your news?"

"I don't know as I want to tell you now," said Chuffy sulkily. "I come in here all happy and all you can do is march up and down like a demned Friday-faced Bengal tiger."

That brought an unwilling smile from the Duke and he sat down. "I have been called a lot of things in my time, Chuffy, but never, until now, a Friday-faced-Bengal tiger. Out with it, man."

"I'm engaged to be married," Chuffy burst out proudly.

The Duke raised his thin eyebrows in surprise. "Married! To whom?"

"Priscilla Wheatcroft."

"Congratulations, Chuffy. You've kept your affairs very quiet. I did not know that you had been seeing much of Miss Wheatcroft."

"Oh, I have been seein' *a lot* of Miss Wheatcroft," said Chuffy with a wicked grin. "Y'know, Henry, she's a most surprising girl. Why you'd never think to look at her that she . . . that she could . . . that she would ever . . . anyway, what I mean is, she's full of surprises."

The Duke smiled but said nothing so Chuffy went on, "Fact is, I was lookin' forward to tellin' Frederica about it all. Why is she in the country?"

"Because I sent her there," said the Duke heavily. For the second time that morning, he found himself telling his story.

Chuffy looked at him goggle-eyed. "Frederica! Consorting with a lot of bucks in a gambling hell! There must be something behind it. Why, Frederica is Mrs. Propriety herself! That's why she liked me as an escort. Knew I was safe and that no one would take it seriously, what with my ridiculous clothes and demned accidents. You know, I haven't had one accident since I changed from the Dandy set. Look! I'm even growing my own hair."

He raised his wig to reveal a head of tiny light brown curls.

The Duke had not even seemed to have noticed Chuffy's new wig. He was sitting back in a high winged chair staring moodily into the flames.

"There was something havey-cavey about that Barnet business," said Chuffy suddenly. The Duke looked up quickly. " 'Member that day when she was crying in St. James's Park and I thought it was because I was borin' her to tears with tales about old Pegasus, y'see, some ladies don't *like* horses. Now that may seem strange to you and it seems downright strange to me. Now take old Pegasus. . . ."

"Chuffy," said the Duke between his teeth, "get on with it."

"Oh, yes, where was I? Ah, I've got it. Well, y'see, before yesterday, I didn't know that much about the gentler sex but now I've got a bit more experience. I think she was cryin' about you chasin' her to Barnet and not about horses."

"That doesn't help me," said the Duke. "On the contrary that leads me to believe that there was something deeper in her relationship with the Comte than I had been led to believe."

"What a pair you are," said Chuffy. "Never seen a marriage like it, beggin' your pardon and all that."

The Duke was opening his mouth to make an angry reply when the butler entered and announced that there was "a woman to see Your Grace."

"What kind of a woman? You know better, Worthing, than to open the door to . . . er . . . never mind, who is it?"

"The person calls herself Mrs. O'Brien."

"She does, does she," said the Duke grimly. "Show her in."

Mrs. O'Brien sailed into the room and sank into a deep curtsy from which she was unable to rise without the assistance of two footmen. "Did I look like that?" asked Chuffy gloomily.

A great wave of patchouli spread itself around the room reminding the Duke vividly of the night of Frederica's disgrace.

"Why have you come?" he asked, levelling his quizzing glass at the huge bulk of the gambling house owner.

"I've come about your dear wife," she wheezed. "I've got something here," she patted a huge reticule, "that I believe will show there was a plot afoot to discredit the Duchess."

"Hand it over!" snapped the Duke.

"Not so fast," said Mrs. O'Brien, clutching her reticule tightly to her massive bosom. "I come out in this dreadful dirty snow all for the sake of your good lady's name. I paid for the hire of that there carriage outside. I . . ."

"How much?"

"One thousand guineas," said Mrs. O'Brien calmly as her large eyes in a face empurpled with the cold took a careful inventory of the furnishings.

"Five hundred," said the Duke, "and not a penny more."

"I'm a poor woman, Your Grace, what with the price of suppers and candles and . . ."

"Four hundred."

"Eight hundred, your dukeship, and the letter is yours."

"Three hundred."

"You're a hard, hard man. A rich aristocutt such as yourself should be prepared to shell out proper for to protect such a sweet angel as his lady wife."

"Be off with you."

"I'll take the five hundred," said Mrs. O'Brien quickly, opening her bag.

She handed over the letter. The Duke smoothed it out and read it carefully.

"Who wrote this?"

"Well, your dukeship, for another few guineas I could . . ."

"Who wrote it, you bloodsucker, or do I have to choke the information out of you?"

"Jack Ferrand," she said sulkily. "I recognized his hand cos' I hold several of his I.O.U.'s. Furthermore, when I asked him what the Duchess was doing at a gambling hell, he like tells me she has the gambling fever and a punshunt for young bucks. I was only trying to supply the demand when you came charging in."

The Duke stood up. "You may go, Mrs. O'Brien."

"But Your Grace, it's an uncommon cold day and I was hoping to moisten my lips with a little something."

The Duke pulled the bell rope hard. "I have never yet struck a woman Mrs. O'Brien, but if you do not take yourself off I shall moisten your lips with the back of my fist. Ah, Worthing, take this person to Mr. Dubble and see that she receives her money." He gave Worthing a note and stood silently looking into the fire until Mrs. O'Brien had gone.

"I'll kill him," he said simply.

"Good," replied Chuffy matter-of-factly. "Let's go. We'll probably find him at Brooks."

The famous Whig club was thin of company, but Jack Ferrand was seated at one of the windows with Archie Hefford and Lord Sackett. All were silent, looking out at the steadily falling snow.

The Duke strode up to their table with Chuffy close behind him. Lord Sackett began to giggle. "How martial you look, dear Chuffy. Is this your new image?" Then his painted mouth fell open in surprise for the Duke of Westerland had removed his York tan gloves and struck Jack Ferrand across the face with them.

"You have plotted and schemed against my wife," said the Duke. "I demand satisfaction."

"You're mad," declared Jack Ferrand with a fixed smile. "I refuse to talk to you. You are quite mad."

The Duke threw Jack Ferrand's glass of wine full in his face. "What do I have to do to make you accept my challenge, you coward?" he demanded. "I believe you are in some way related to me, which makes it worse. You are a disgrace to the Westerland family."

"I'll meet you. And God in Heaven, I'll kill you," hissed Jack Ferrand. "How dare you say I am not worthy of the Westerlands. Were it not for you, you miserable crawling half-pay Captain, I would be the Duke. *I* would hold the title. Not you. Yes, I will kill you. Did you think I would stand by and see you father brats by that common little slut you married . . . stand by and see them take *my* title. Name your seconds."

Chuffy and Archie Hefford promptly volunteered to second the Duke and Lord Sackett, twittering with excitement, said he would act for Mr. Ferrand and that his friend, Mr. Gordon, who was shortly due to arrive, would act as well.

They silently elected to walk, each one trudging through the sooty snow of London, each one wrapped in his own thoughts. Chuffy was the first to speak. "They say Jack Ferrand's a good man with a sword."

"So am I," remarked the Duke and both fell silent again. Melting snowflakes ran down his face like tears and glinted on his snowy cravat. Fear and worry for his little wife consumed him. He remembered all her shy and hesitant approaches and how he had brutally snubbed her, hiding his hurt feelings behind a chilly mask of formality. Then he stopped stock still while Chuffy ambled aimlessly round him in the snow like a pet dog.

"Clarissa!" cried the Duke. "She must

have been a part of this plot. She told me about Mrs. O'Brien's." He swung off in the direction of Clarence Square with Chuffy trotting at his heels.

Mrs. Sayers and Clarissa were seated over their needlework in the drawing room and both fluttered to their feet as the Duke strode into the room followed by Chuffy.

"I would beg a word with you in private, Miss Sayers," said the Duke, pointedly holding open the door for Mrs. Sayers.

But Mrs. Sayers stood her ground. "I am tired of being ordered out of my own drawing room," she snapped, all poses from the girlish to the languid fled to reveal the tough and brutal north country woman underneath.

But Clarissa was made of stronger stuff than even her formidable mother. Her eyes had flashed to the Duke's face and from the look in his eyes, she feared the game was up. There may yet be a way to save the day but only by getting rid of her mother.

"Go, mama," she ordered.

"I'll not go, my lass. Ah'll stay reet here alongt you and his nibs," said Mrs. Sayers, her normally refined accents disappearing in a burst of rage.

Clarissa flew at her like a wild cat. "Get out of here, you stupid woman. You make me sick!" She gave her mother a stinging slap across the face. Mrs. Sayers began to scream but the undaunted Clarissa tugged the bell and ordered the butler to summon madame's maid on the double.

All three waited in silence as Mrs. Sayers' noisy sobs could be heard disappearing up the stairs and along the corridor to her room.

Clarissa turned to the gentlemen with a light laugh. "You must forgive my dramatics. I fear mama needs a strong hand to control her."

"So, it seems, do you," said the Duke moving towards her. She backed away before the fury in his face.

"I have just discovered that Jack Ferrand has been plotting against my wife. He sent her a note to lure her to a certain Mrs. O'Brien's. Now it was you who so touchingly told me that I would find Frederica there. What do you have to say to that?"

Clarissa thought quickly. He obviously did not know of her complicity, else why would he ask? She gave him a tremulous smile and said, "How horrible! I never did like that man. Poor little Freddie! My dear Henry, it was, of course, Mr. Ferrand who told me all about Frederica's going to Mrs. O'Brien's gambling house and suggested that I tell you. He was so convincing that I did not suspect a plot. Oh, please believe me."

Her beautiful mouth was trembling and her large eyes shone with tears. The Duke could see no trace of deceit on her face.

"Very well, Clarissa," he said heavily. "It appears that you have been tricked the same as I. Come Chuffy."

After they had left, Clarissa sat alone for a long time wondering when it would all end. She was sure the Duke would challenge Jack Ferrand to a duel if he had not already done so. She was soon to receive her answer.

Jack Ferrand burst into the drawing room without even pausing to remove his snow-covered benjamin. "Have you heard from Westerland?" he asked coming to stand over her.

"Yes," said Clarissa, barely able to conceal her fear and dislike.

"Does he know of your part in this?"

Clarissa shook her head.

"Good! You will do one more thing for me. The Duke is meeting me to fight a duel at Chalk Farm at five in the morning. You must alert the authorities and have the duel stopped."

Clarissa surveyed him with contempt. "You are frightened of Henry."

"Do as I say and spare me your insults," he snapped.

"Oh, very well," sighed Clarissa.

But after he had gone, she stared out of the window as he climbed into his carriage. A slow smile curved her lips. "No, I shall not alert the authorities, Mr. Ferrand. I hope to God he kills you."

The first thing the Duke did on his return to Grosvenor Square was to send for his steward, Benjamin Dubble. He explained as briefly as possible that his wife was alone at Chartsay and, because he was unable to leave town due to a pressing engagement, he wished Mr. Dubble to ride poste-haste and bring her back.

"I shall give you a letter . . ." he began and then paused. There was too much to say. What if he were killed? "No," he said slowly. "On second thoughts, do not bring her back. Tell her I shall be joining her to-morrow. Take Entwhistle, my secretary, with you. Should any accident befall me, I shall leave a letter for the Duchess on my desk."

Benjamin Dubble hesitated. "I don't know if we shall manage to reach Chartsay, today, Your Grace. I fear the roads will be blocked."

"Do your best," he said wearily. "And Dubble . . ."

"Yes, Your Grace."

"If my wife is experiencing any embarrassment or difficulty with Lawton, give him his marching orders."

"*Certainly,* Your Grace," said Dubble, his face creasing in a smile.

The Duke was left alone to draw forward several sheets of letter paper and to stare down at them, seeing only the image of Frederica's face. What if she did not love him? What if he were too late?

The weary winter day stretched on as he searched for the correct phrases to explain what was in his heart in case he should not return alive from Chalk Farm. Sheet after sheet of paper was crumpled and torn up as he slaved over the delicate task of explaining to his wife that he had fallen head over heels in love with her: that, in retrospect, he must have been in love with her for a long time. Finally as the parish lamps were lit in the square outside and the butlers stood out on the steps of the various households to exchange gossip and take the evening air, he finally finished by confining himself to a few simple and direct sentences.

A weight suddenly seemed to have been lifted from his soul. There was nothing left to do but retire to bed and pray that he would acquit himself honorably on the morrow.

But just before he closed his eyes, he decided that he would fight as he had never fought before to avenge all the heartbreak and shame that Jack Ferrand had caused his little wife.

His little wife was, at that moment, settling down to sleep and planning vengeance of her own. Despite the loyal servants, the pompous Lawton and his sister had managed to make the great mansion thrum with an atmosphere of hate and venom. Foul practical jokes had been the order of the day, culminating in the presentation of a covered dish on the dinner table which, when opened, had revealed a live rat. She could not flee for even the loyal members of the staff knew of the Duke's ruling and would not go so far as to let her make her escape. Tomorrow, she decided, in some way she would trap Lawton. All she needed to do was to bait the trap. She lay on her pillows staring out at the snow swirling outside the windows and tried not to think of her husband. All her troubles had really begun the day she was locked in the ice house. The ice house! She sat bolt upright as a plan began to form in her head.

She rang the bell and summoned her maid.

Benson found her mistress already getting dressed. "Quickly, Benson," said Frederica turning round to the sleepy maid. "You must somehow get me the key to the ice house."

Benson yawned, "That's easy, Your Grace. After all the trouble there was last time about you being locked in, I remember one of the servants saying that anyone could have got hold of the key seeing as how it was hanging on a nail in the stillroom." Then she came fully awake and stared at Frederica. "Whatever does Your Grace want with a key at this time of night?"

"Don't ask questions," said Frederica imperiously. "Bring it to me immediately and make sure that every servant you meet knows that I am going to lock my jewels in the ice house. You will say that I do not trust Lawton and that I fear he means to rob me. No! Don't argue with me. Go directly."

Benson went off grumbling to change her clothes and collect the key. She returned some time later with an even gloomier look on her face. "I hope you know what you're doing, ma'am. All Lawton's lot was hanging around with their eyes popping out of their heads."

"All the better," said Frederica. "Help me on with my pattens."

When she was finally well wrapped up, she gave her heavy jewel box to the maid and together they quietly crept from the apartment.

The snow had stopped falling and a small winter's moon raced high above.

The world looked as if it had been washed clean and the very act of taking some sort of action made Frederica's heart lighter. Benson struggled along behind her, her long skirts hampering her progress through the snow. "Ma'am!" she whispered to Frederica. "There's always duplicates of these keys and the Groom of the Chambers has them all."

"I know," said Frederica simply. Their heavy skirts and wooden pattens left a long trail stretching behind them to the house. Frederica looked behind her with satisfaction. "There are no clear prints," she murmured. "If we wait long enough, they will think we have returned to the house."

Benson opened her mouth, shut it again and rolled her eyes heavenwards instead. Frederica unlocked the door of the ice house and pushed it open, looking into the dark depths of the interior with a shudder as she remembered her imprisonment. She lit the stub of a candle at the door. "You stay outside and see that no one comes," she whispered to Benson. She crawled slowly along the tunnel to the edge of the vault and left the heavy jewel box on the ground and retreated quickly so as not to rouse the bats.

"Go back to the house and enter by the terrace. I have left the window open," she said. "If anyone asks for me, say that I returned before you and went to bed. They will think that they have missed me. Go *on*," she added, giving the wide-eyed maid a little push. "Hurry!"

Benson scurried off whimpering to herself. But her years in service had taught her not to question the whims and ways of the quality.

Left alone, Frederica dug herself a small cave in a snow bank near the entrance to the ice house and sat down to wait, too excited to feel the cold.

After a time, she heard footsteps creaking in the powdery snow, surprisingly close, and Lawton's voice whispered, "Stop grumbling. I tell you the Duke is so mad at her that he will not believe one word she says. He'll probably think that she pawned the jewels to get money for her gambling. I had the whole story from the coachman before he left. The Duke, I told you, found her in that gambling hell. Says he wished he'd never married her. Said it as clear as day."

"I don't trust that one," came Mrs. Lawton's whisper.

"Stow it," said Lawton rudely. "You'll be able to buy yourself a husband." Like all housekeepers, Rebecca Lawton had the honorary title of 'Mrs.' although she was a spinster of fifty-four.

Frederica heard him fumbling for the key and suddenly realized that her plan was about to fall apart. Lawton would carry the key into the ice house with him. All she could do was to scream and accuse them of the theft. They had disappeared into the tunnel as she emerged and the first thing she saw was the frosty moonlight shining on the key in the door. Stumbling over the snow, she threw herself on the door, slammed it shut and locked it.

She was in time to hear a muffled cry of rage and disappointment from Lawton. The Groom of the Chambers had obviously just opened the jewel box.

With a smile of satisfaction, Frederica sped lightly away, seeming to skim along over the top of the snow. Benson was waiting for her in her bedroom still looking wide-eyed into a drawer in the dresser.

"I was looking for a fresh nightrobe

and . . . and I found this —" Lying in the drawer were all Frederica's jewels, the ruby collar, the Westerland diamonds, all blazing and flashing in the candlelight. "What was in the box, ma'am?" asked Benson.

"Rocks. Ordinary stones," said Frederica calmly. "I got them from the garden while you were looking for the key."

"And Lawton . . . ?"

"Lawton and his awful sister are locked in the ice house."

"What if they die? When do you mean to let them out?"

"Oh, I won't let them out . . . but the other servants will. They won't have told their cronies what they planned to do but since other servants know about the jewels, it will not be long before they guess where to find Lawton and the housekeeper. That horrible pair of bullies will just have to spend a miserable night. I plan to make their lives every bit as miserable as they plan to make mine. Send the knife boy to me first thing in the morning."

Benson went off shaking her head but Frederica was too excited over winning her first battle to sleep. She could hardly think of her husband except in that painful corner of her brain where his cold voice repeated over and over again, "I wish I had never married you."

As a pale dawn crept across the wintry landscape and a strong easterly wind began to blow the fine snow into spinning columns which weaved among the trees like so many wintry dancing dervishes, Frederica at last fell into a fitful sleep.

Henry, Duke of Westerland, struggled awake and dressed himself quickly without rousing his valet, Stubbs.

His anger of the day before had not abated one whit, and as he edged his horse through the heavy snow in the direction of the fields at Chalk Farm he was followed by the ever faithful Chuffy who had been waiting for him as he descended the stairs that morning.

Chuffy had spent a sleepless night tortured by noble thoughts. He was delighted with his engagement to Priscilla and he felt obscurely that he owed it all to the Duke and Frederica. If it had not been for Frederica, he would not have learned how to be easy in a young lady's company. If it had not been for the friendship of the Duke, he would never had left the Dandy set and would never have felt bold enough to handle Priscilla the way he did. 'Course he hadn't meant to rape her, just teach her a lesson, but, well, things had suddenly got deliciously out of hand on both sides.

Chuffy longed to be able to fight Jack Ferrand himself. Perhaps he could make the Duke have an accident, but as he looked at the Duke's tall athletic figure riding in front of him he realized that if he did anything to stop the duel, he never would be forgiven.

The white fields of Chalk Farm were spread out in sleepy silence under their blanket of snow. The surgeon arrived in a hack, a clock in a neighboring steeple began to strike five, and there was no sign of Jack Ferrand. He did not mean to come, thought Chuffy, and heaved a sigh of relief.

"He ain't comin', Henry," he said, edging his horse nearer the Duke's. "I know a cosy little inn where we can have a spanking breakfast."

The Duke stayed rigid on his horse without replying, his hard eyes constantly raked over the snowy field. Archie Hefford, Lord Sackett, and Mr. Gordon arrived together but still there was no sign of Jack Ferrand. The steeple clock mournfully struck the quarter past and a faint grey line of light appeared on the horizon.

"He isn't coming," said Archie Hefford at last. "Come along, Henry. We'll hunt him down in London."

"Wait!" said the Duke.

A solitary horseman was riding towards them.

Jack Ferrand was desperately looking for the officers of the law. He had given them plenty of time to get there. As he rode across the field, he suddenly realized that Clarissa had done nothing in the hope that he would be killed.

Coats were removed, swords were presented, the antagonists faced each other, and Chuffy turned his back.

"Hey! You're one of the seconds. Turn around," cried Archie Hefford.

"I can't watch," said Chuffy, the tears forming in his eyes. "Best friend I ever had."

"You're a Corinthian now," said Archie, moved by the big man's distress. "You've got to see there's fair play."

Chuffy dried his eyes and turned round as the duel began. It became evident from the first that both men were out to kill. Ferrand was an expert and at times the Duke was hard pressed. But Ferrand's hate and temper began to get the better of him as his tall opponent skillfully parried every move and he lashed and hacked, his feet sliding on the treacherous ground.

Suddenly, the Duke missed his own footing and half slipped down into the snow. Jack Ferrand leapt down on him with a tremendous thrust and Chuffy closed his eyes. But Archie Hefford, watching intently, saw the Duke twist away from the glittering point and strike upwards.

There was a long silence and when Chuffy opened his eyes, Jack Ferrand's body was lying on the snow, his blood staining the white a deep crimson. The Duke was turning away when he heard a hoarse whisper, "Westerland!" He moved back and looked down at the wounded man who was raising himself up on one elbow. "Clarissa!" whispered Jack Ferrand. "She was in the plot with me . . . with me all along." His voice trailed away and he fell back unconscious. The surgeon bustled forward opening his instrument case. After a long inspection, he raised his head. "He'll live, gentlemen."

"Good," said the Duke. "It is not worth fleeing the country because of vermin like this. Take him away."

Lord Sackett minced forward holding a scented lace handkerchief to his nose. "My dear Duke," he twittered. "I assure you, I was wise to Mr. Ferrand all along. Horrid man. Never cared for him and furthermore . . ." But that was as far as he got. Chuffy relieved his pent-up feelings by punching Lord Sackett with a flush hit on the nose.

Chuffy put an arm round the Duke's shoulders. "Get your coat on, Henry, and we'll have that breakfast."

The Duke shrugged him off. "First of all," he said, "I have a call to pay on Miss Clarissa Sayers."

Chapter Thirteen

Clarissa put down her cup of chocolate with exaggerated care as she heard the commotion in the corridor outside. She knew the game was up.

The door crashed open and the Duke of Westerland and Chuffy strode into the room. Mrs. Sayers followed after them, threatening and screaming.

"You assault my servants and break into my daughter's bedroom. I shall call Bow Street."

"Call out the army for all I care," said the Duke indifferently. "You obviously do not care if the whole world hears of your daughter's perfidy."

Clarissa pulled a wrapper round herself and climbed down from her bed and stood before them. "Go away, mama," she said in a tired voice.

"Have you gone mad?" screamed Mrs. Sayers.

"Then stay," said Clarissa indifferently. "It's a good story. You should enjoy it."

Not looking at the Duke, she began to tell

her story in a cold hard voice. She told baldly of her jealousy of Frederica, how Jack Ferrand had threatened her at gunpoint and then promised to tell the whole of London he had lain with her if she did not do what he asked.

She neither cried nor fluttered not tried to excuse herself.

"It did not seem so great a thing, after all," she said, turning her eyes at last to the Duke. "I was not hurting Frederica's heart after all, only her reputation. I am beautiful but I am courted for my money. My money will buy me a title and that is the way the world goes. Is it not so, mama?"

Mrs. Sayers moaned and closed her eyes.

"So," went on Clarissa, "what kind of revenge do you plan? Tell London and it will cause a scandal in the family and all for what? Love? It does not exist."

The Duke felt sick. Clarissa, telling the truth for the first time in her life, was more frightening than the charming and lying Clarissa he had known before. Even her beauty seemed only a wax mask.

He turned to Mrs. Sayers. "We will have no more of this fiction of Frederica being your daughter. She is your stepdaughter. You will neither see nor speak to her again. Either of you. Come Chuffy."

The two men strode from the room leaving Clarissa and her mother facing each other. At last Clarissa turned an indifferent shoulder and climbed into bed. Mrs. Sayers opened her mouth to say something but was forestalled by her daughter. "I am what you made me," said Clarissa in a cold, thin voice. "You will have a lord as a son-in-law. Do not expect anything else. You cannot breed the softer sympathies out of me and then be surprised."

"They were not bred out of Frederica," whispered Mrs. Sayers.

"A miracle, isn't it?" laughed Clarissa. "What an absolute miracle."

Mrs. Sayers gave her indifferent daughter one terrified look and then left the room.

But if Mrs. Sayers could have seen her stepdaughter at that moment, she would have judged Frederica to have lost all of the softer sympathies. As the great house was in an uproar over the disappearance of the Lawtons she sat unmoved at her embroidery frame with a still, cold expression which seemed at odds with her youthful appearance.

Benson ushered the small knife boy into the room and he stood with his head bowed, wondering why such an exalted a personage as the Duchess had summoned him.

"What is your name, boy?" asked Frederica putting down her needle.

"Jem," he whispered. "Jem Cartwright."

"Well, Jem, I have asked you here because you seem to be a bright boy. Do you like practical jokes?"

Jem searched his brain frantically, wondering if he had made any recent misdemeanor, and, realizing his conscience was clear, raised his head and said, "I ain't done nuffink, Your Grace."

"No, I am sure you have not," said Frederica. "But I asked to see you in the hope that you might have a talent for practical joking." This was said in a quiet pleasant voice and Jem looked up at her with a gleam of interest in his eyes.

"You see," went on Frederica, picking up her needle again, "the Lawtons appear to be lost but I feel sure that they will return shortly. I am sure Mrs. Lawton would appreciate some sort of welcome."

"That 'un don't deserve no welcome," said Jem roundly, and then the light began to dawn. "Or does Your Grace mean a kind of joke welcome?"

"Exactly! What a bright boy you are to be sure," said Frederica calmly.

Jem's eyes began to sparkle. "Well, Mrs.

Lawton's mortal affeard of birds, Your Grace. Anything with feathers scares her. Why, she won't even go near the kitchens when they's plucking the birds."

"Very well, Jem. I feel sure I can leave it to you to visit Mrs. Lawton's room and arrange a welcome. You will be suitably rewarded, of course."

"Getting even with that old quiz is the only reward I need," said Jem stoutly. "But if you was to let me take some food home to me Mum, it would be helpful, like."

"A whole hamper," said Frederica, suddenly grinning at him and looking the same age as the mischievous knife boy. "Be off with you."

"Oh, ma'am, aren't you scared?" cried Benson after the boy had left.

"Not a bit of it," said Frederica. "If I had not been such a weakling before perhaps I should not be in this fix. I should have fought to keep my marriage." Her voice broke, "Now my husband is probably passing the time at his club and considers he is well rid of me."

Her husband, on the contrary, was at that moment riding hell for leather towards Chartsay, followed by the faithful Chuffy.

The Duke was glad that they had taken

their horses instead of the carriage which would never have managed to get through the deeply-rutted roads.

As far as the eye could see, the snowy fields flashed and dazzled under the winter sun and they seemed to be the only moving figures on the wintry landscape.

They galloped round a bend in the road and drew rein beside a light travelling vehicle which was upended in a ditch. "Halloa!" said the Duke. "Some traveller's come to grief." He drew closer and his lips tightened in a grim line. "By all that's holy, that's one of my travelling carriages. Something must have happened to Entwhistle and Dubble."

They rode slowly on, looking for any sign of the steward and secretary. As they rounded another bend in the country road, they espied a small inn which seemed to be huddled down in the ditch. The Duke dismounted and strode into the tap, calling loudly for the landlord.

He was met instead by his secretary, James Entwhistle, who was descending the stairs and whose face lit up with relief when he saw his master.

"Oh, Your Grace," he cried. "You must forgive me for not proceeding to Chartsay. We were overturned on the road and Mr. Dubble broke his leg and is now in a high fever. I did not like to leave him."

"You did well," said the Duke, fighting down a sudden qualm of anxiety for his wife. He rapidly mounted the stairs and pushed open the low door of a bedroom under the thatch. The landlord's wife, who had been sitting beside the bed, rose to her feet at his entrance and made a low curtsy. "The fever is less," she whispered. "I think he should not be moved."

The elderly steward looked very small and frail on the bed. His face was very flushed and he turned his head restlessly from side to side in his sleep.

"Have you sent for the doctor?" asked the Duke, turning abruptly to Mr. Entwhistle.

"Yes, Your Grace. The landlord left as soon as the road was relatively clear."

"Then you had better wait for him. I must ride on to Chartsay. I am concerned for my wife. I shall send several of the servants back with a heavy carriage and as soon as the fever has abated, have Mr. Dubble conveyed to Chartsay."

The Duke's face was drawn and worried as he remounted his horse and spurred on down the road. He should never have left Frederica alone with servants such as the Lawtons. They were probably bullying the life out of her. . . .

★ ★ ★

The Lawtons had been discovered in the ice house as Frederica had predicted. The fact that they intended to keep the jewels to themselves had alienated even their closest cronies and they found scant sympathy for their shivering state. Lawton retired to the kitchen to put his feet in a mustard bath, Mrs. Lawton to her room.

The shivering housekeeper pushed open her door. When she had thawed out, she would go downstairs directly and put Her Grace, the Duchess of Westerland, to the rightabout. No little upstart jade was going to get the better of her. No . . .

She froze on the threshold of her room as hundreds of pairs of eyes stared back at her. The knife boy had surpassed himself. There were hens on the mantel shelf and ducks on the bed. A brace of pheasants stared at her curiously from the armchair and several pigeons roosted on the windowsill. The floor was covered with cackling, hissing, and screeching birds — a feathery sea of geese, hens, pigeons, grouse and pheasants. Mrs. Lawton screamed and screamed as the whole feathery flock disturbed by the noise rose as one bird to make their escape. Screaming and flailing her arms, she backed along the corridor as the heavy flap of wings beat about her head.

She ran headlong down the main staircase . . . and then stopped.

The Duchess of Westerland was standing at the foot of the stairs, looking up at her with a cold hard stare. Mrs. Lawton suddenly realized that she was as much terrified of the little Duchess as she was of the squawking, flapping birds and sank down on the stairs and burst into tears.

The servants had all come running into the hall, drawn by her frantic screams. Some ran about trying to catch the birds, some fell back before the small figure of the Duchess and tried to disappear back to the kitchen quarters, and other members of the female staff stood and screamed and held up their skirts.

The great door crashed open and the Duke and Chuffy stood on the threshold, looking as if they couldn't believe their eyes.

Frederica came to life. "Oh, Chuffy, I am *so* glad you are come," she cried, throwing herself into the large gentleman's arms. Chuffy rolled his eyes towards the Duke for help and the Duke gently disengaged Frederica's arms from Chuffy, feeling desolately that he had indeed left things too late.

"Chuffy! Go and find out who is behind this rumpus and dismiss who you will. I must talk to my wife."

Chuffy hurried off and the Duke kept a firm hold of Frederica who was trying to break away. He led her into the long drawing room, noticing with fury that it was as cold as the day outside and that the hearth was black and empty.

He drew the struggling girl onto his knee on one of the Chesterfields and held her hands. "Frederica," he said. "Please listen to me. I was wrong. Wrong all along. It was Jack Ferrand who was trying to come between us. And I was so angry because . . . because I love you so much."

Frederica became suddenly still. "My dear," he went on. "I will not force myself on you. I said it should be a marriage of convenience and so it shall remain, if you wish it. I certainly did not think I should fall in love . . . but there it is."

They sat motionless. He was frightened to look at her face. The setting sun blazed across the snow outside and lit the enormous room with a fiery glow. Frederica gently laid her head on his shoulder like a weary child. "I love you so much," she whispered. "I began to think you would never love me back. In fact I began to think you hated me. . . ." His lips closed over hers as the fiery sunset died away and long shadows began to creep across the room.

At last she drew away a little and began to tell him her story in a faltering voice, of her escape from the Comte, of the fear she once had that he wanted to divorce her and marry Clarissa.

"Clarissa!" he cried, pulling her into his arms again. "That hell cat was working for Jack Ferrand. You shall never see her again, Frederica."

Frederica gave a little sigh of relief and turned her face up to his. His kisses became more violent and both found that they were beginning to tremble with passion and cold.

He released her and laughed. "What a curst cold place to make love. Come let us find somewhere warmer."

She shyly put her hand in his and he led her towards the door.

Chuffy had dismissed the Lawtons but they were waiting outside the door to plead their case with the Duke who would surely not listen to a wife he so despised.

The drawing room door swung open and the Duke and Duchess emerged, gazing into each others' eyes. Like sleepwalkers they moved slowly across the hall towards their private apartments.

When they had disappeared, Chuffy grinned at the Lawtons. "Well, there's your answer." With bowed heads, the Lawtons left to attend to their packing.

Chuffy ate his dinner that evening in a solitary state as neither the Duke nor the Duchess showed any signs of joining him.

Later he leaned his large elbows on his windowsill to breathe in the cold night air. The rumble of a masculine voice came from Frederica's room, which was beneath his. It was answered by a rippling laugh from Frederica. Chuffy had never heard her sound so happy. With one great sentimental sigh, he closed the window, blew out the candle and climbed into bed.

About the Author

Born in Glasgow, Scotland, Ms. Chesney started her writing career while working as a fiction buyer in a bookstore in Glasgow. She doubled as a theater critic, newspaper reporter, and editor before coming to the United States in 1971. She later returned to London, where she lives with her husband and one child near Kensington Palace.

We hope you have enjoyed this Large Print book. Other Thorndike Press or Chivers Press Large Print books are available at your library or directly from the publishers.

For more information about current and upcoming titles, please call or write, without obligation, to:

Thorndike Press
P.O. Box 159
Thorndike, Maine 04986 USA
Tel. (800) 223-1244
Tel. (800) 223-6121

OR

Chivers Press Limited
Windsor Bridge Road
Bath BA2 3AX
England
Tel. (0225) 335336

All our Large Print titles are designed for easy reading, and all our books are made to last.